☆ ALASKA

ALASKA

Luree Miller & Scott Miller

COBBLEHILL BOOKS

Pioneer Stories of a
Twentieth-Century Frontier

Illustrated with photographs & maps

DUTTON ★ New York

The publisher gratefully acknowledges permission to reprint the quotations on:

Page 72, reproduced by permission of McGraw-Hill from *The Highliners: A Documentary Novel About the Fishermen of Alaska* by William B. McCloskey, Jr., © 1981, page 6.

Page 47, reproduced by permission of the Smithsonian Institution Press from *Inua: Spirit World of the Bering Sea Eskimo*, "The Way They Lived Long Ago," William Fitzhugh (ed.) © Smithsonian Institution, Washington, D.C. 1982.

Library of Congress Cataloging-in-Publication Data
Miller, Luree.
   Alaska : pioneer stories of a twentieth-century frontier / Luree
Miller and Scott Miller.
   p.   cm.
   Includes bibliographical references and index.
   Summary: Explores the epic struggle of Alaska pioneer families and their quest to exploit and develop the resources of America's great bastion to the North.
   ISBN 0-525-65050-4
   1. Frontier and pioneer life—Alaska—Juvenile literature.
2. Pioneers—Alaska—Biography—Juvenile literature. 3. Alaska—Social life and customs—Juvenile literature. [1. Frontier and pioneer life—Alaska. 2. Alaska—History.] I. Miller, Scott, 1950- . II. Title.
F909.M57 1991
979.8—dc20   91-10744 CIP AC

Published in the United States by Cobblehill Books, an affiliate of Dutton Children's Books, a division of Penguin Books USA Inc.

Designed by Charlotte Staub
Printed in the United States of America   First Edition
10 9 8 7 6 5 4 3 2 1

To the memory of

B I L L Y   M I L L E R

Born in Alaska,
where his heart
remained

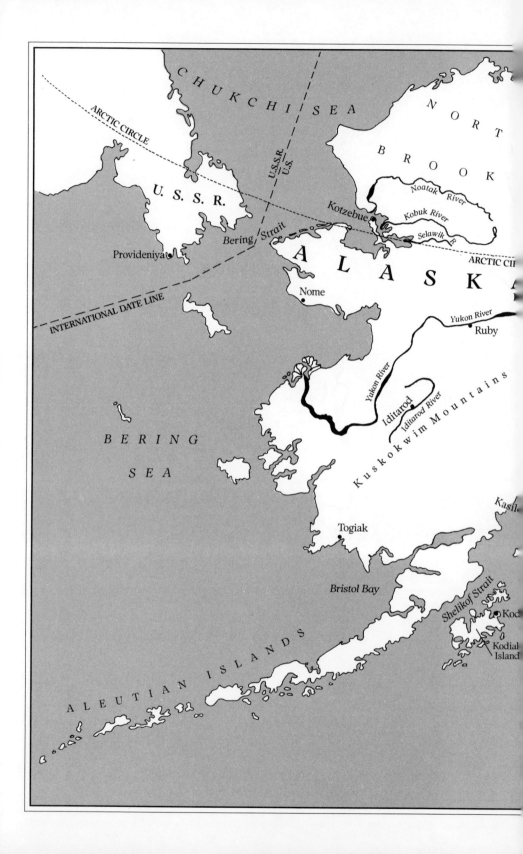

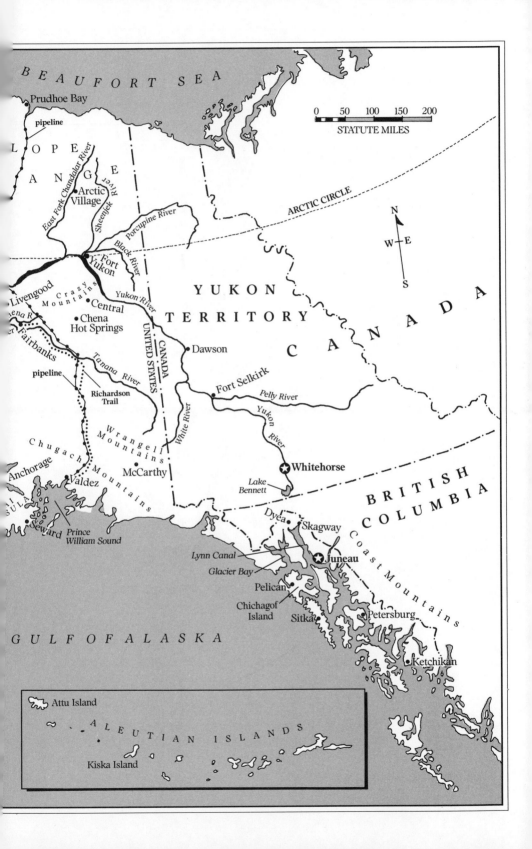

 # CONTENTS

☆ AUTHORS' NOTE

Our hearts and lives have long been entangled with Alaska and we are deeply grateful to our Alaskan family and friends who made this book possible. Their stories informed and inspired us. They are part of the heritage of a rapidly changing Alaska and we felt they should not be lost to history.

Not only the subjects of this book, but their families and friends as well, spent long hours talking to us, going through family papers and pictures, and doublechecking facts to confirm their memories. To all of them our heartfelt thanks for their tireless cooperation.

From the beginning we have been indebted to Brent Ashabranner, who first suggested that we collaborate on this book. His criticism and sense of history spurred us on.

☆ SEWARD'S FOLLY

Alaska derives its name from an Aleut word meaning "The Great Land," and no state is better named. It is over twice the size of the next largest state, Texas. This is a sore point for Texans, and Alaskans like to tease them: in a favorite Alaskan joke Alaska threatens to divide itself in two to make Texas the third largest state.

Superimpose a map of Alaska over a map of the rest of the United States. From the tip of its long Aleutian Island chain to the end of its southeast panhandle, Alaska stretches over the length from the West to the East coasts. From Barrow in the north to the curve of the Aleutians, Alaska reaches the distance from Canada to Mexico.

Alaska is vast in scale, in time as well as space. It is the place where man first set foot on the uninhabited American

_____

continent, between 35,000 and 14,000 years ago, when the Russian and American mainlands were connected by a land bridge over what is now the Bering Sea. For uncounted centuries, scattered Native races mastered this fierce environment.

Alaska's encounters with the West began with the Russian expedition of Vitus Bering in 1741. Attracted by the profitable fur trade, Russia colonized Alaska and enslaved the Aleuts. Remains of over a century of Russian rule and occupation can be found today along the southern coast of Alaska, including onion-domed Russian Orthodox churches.

When Alaska was purchased from the Czar of Russia in 1867, the $7 million investment was not greatly valued by most Americans. Secretary of State William Seward saw his acquisition mocked as "a frozen desert of a colony" and "Seward's Folly." The huge new territory was home to 29,000 Eskimos, Aleuts, Tlingits, and Athapaskans, and 1,000 whites.

Until the end of the nineteenth century, Alaska was virtually ignored by the rest of the country. For its first seventeen years under U.S. control, it was simply designated as a customs district. Laws and government were introduced gradually, as needs arose.

Then in 1896, there was a rich gold strike in the Klondike in Yukon Territory, Canada, right next to Alaska and chiefly accessible across the Alaskan coastal panhandle. And in 1898 more quantities of gold were discovered on the other side of Alaska, on the remote coast of the Bering Sea near Nome.

News of these strikes fired the imaginations of men around the world. Alaska was seen as a land of golden dreams and fabulous wealth. As the twentieth century dawned, Alaska had entered the American consciousness as the last frontier. It did not become an organized territory until 1912.

Alaska is still America's modern pioneer state. Throughout

the twentieth century, Alaska has been the scene of frontier adventure and conflict. Most of the American West was explored and settled at the turn of the century. Alaska's development as part of the United States had just begun.

For most of the twentieth century, Alaska was a land district and then a territory. It took until 1920 to finally finish surveying its boundary with Canada. Alaska was not admitted to the Union as the forty-ninth state until 1959. Then it became the largest state in size and the smallest in population. Since statehood, the number of people in Alaska has more than doubled, to approximately half a million, still less than most large American cities.

The relatively small number of Alaska's inhabitants face a huge, unspoiled wilderness. Throughout this century, Alaska has seen, on a vast scale, the frontier struggles of booms and busts, development and conservation, ancient Alaskan Native values and headlong modernization, natural and man-made disasters. The land dominates those who live there.

The epic of Alaska in the twentieth century is illustrated by the stories of modern pioneers. These are the men and women who found in Alaska the resources, the space, and the freedom for a way of life that fully challenged them. Whether they came from Outside (anywhere except Alaska) or were born there, Alaska offered them opportunities that existed nowhere else.

For Alaska is a state of mind, as well as a landscape. The qualities of independence, frankness, openness, and self-reliance are prized. In Alaska there is a willingness to accept newcomers, whatever their backgrounds, who seek a new start. In the face of a sometimes overwhelming environment, all members of a community are important.

Some of the major themes of twentieth-century Alaskan life are traced in this book through the stories of notable individuals. The Miller family arrived near the turn of the century looking for gold, but found a way of life that was more important. The Dodsons pioneered the new aviation business in Alaska during the 1930s and 1940s and became a lifeline to people living in the Bush (any remote area without connecting roads and accessible only by boat or plane).

Out of a traditional Eskimo community, Willie Hensley grew up to become an important leader in the Native land rights movement, a bank president, and the president of a large Native corporation. Born and raised in Valdez, Marty Rutherford as a little girl survived the terror of the great 1964 earthquake there and now travels the length and breadth of Alaska, serving small communities as a state official.

Teen-aged Faith Van De Putte grew up on a boat and, with her family, fishes every season in the rich commercial harvest of southeast Alaskan waters. Young, versatile Scott Reymiller and Carol Gelvin-Reymiller live and trap in Bush Alaska near the Arctic Circle, running their dogsled along their traplines when they are not working in the North Slope oil fields or custom-fitting Bush airplanes or going on an archaeological dig.

In this most overpopulated and urbanized of centuries, Alaska is a reminder that people still face frontiers. Our Alaskan pioneers recall to us that America began in small settlements in the wilderness.

FRANK & MARY MILLER:
Gold! The Call of the North

"Gold! We leapt from our benches.
  Gold! We sprang from our stools.
Gold! We wheeled in the furrow, fired with the faith of fools.
Fearless, unfound, unfitted, far from the night and the cold,
Heard we the clarion summons,
    followed the master-lure—Gold!"
                            —"The Trail of Ninety-Eight"
                            Robert Service

Gold—in America! Its lure set young men as far away as Europe dreaming of adventure and a richer life in a frontier land. Stories of the California gold rush of 1849 got better in the retelling. Some even said that the streets in America were paved with gold.

Then, at the end of the 1800s, news exploded of another fabulous gold rush in the Canadian Yukon, quickly followed by more gold discoveries in Alaska.

This dream of gold led one young Slovene from Austria deep into the wilderness of Alaska's last frontier. But Frank Miller's long journey, like those of many other adventurous men and women, was full of trials, disappointments, and then unexpected fulfillment. When Frank finally settled in the heart of Alaska, as an adventurer turned pioneer, something more than gold held him in the far north. It was a feeling of awe for the wild, open landscape and the undreamed-of freedom he found there to build a new life in an uncrowded, undeveloped land.

In the 1880s, when Frank was a young man in his teens, the Emperor of Austria-Hungary was the ruler of his country, Slovenia, which now is part of Yugoslavia. Frank, whose Slovene name was Franc Trsič, lived in the mountain village of Begunje in the Slovene Alps. Franc was a restless young man, short and wiry, quick of movement and very strong. With his piercing blue eyes and handlebar mustache, he cut a dashing figure. Soon he would be drafted into the Austrian army to be a soldier for the Emperor.

But Franc heard that all over Europe young men like himself, who were full of ambition and did not want to serve in the armies of kings, were emigrating to America. Priests in village churches read aloud letters from America describing the freedom in this new land. One reported: "We tip our hats to no one. No king or emperor has the right to command us to do anything."

In the Slovene Alps and the rest of Europe, peasant farms were small and unproductive. So young men like Franc and his brothers had to leave home to find work. If they went to America, they reasoned, they might find gold and riches as well as the freedom they dreamed of.

So in 1886, when Franc Trsič was twenty-two, he and his two younger brothers set out for this fabled land. At Trieste, a port on the Mediterranean Sea, they boarded a small steamship to cross the Atlantic Ocean. Arriving in New York, they were cleared through the U.S. Immigration Service inspection on Ellis Island and made the long train trip across the American continent to Anaconda in western Montana.

Here they found a new, prosperous town in a valley surrounded by wooded hills. Anaconda had been founded only three years earlier by the Anaconda Mining Company, which owned one of the richest copper mines in the world at nearby Butte. Immigrant workers were welcomed by the mining company and there already was a small Slovene community in Anaconda when the Trsič brothers arrived. They quickly found jobs as laborers.

In 1893 Franc married a Slovenian girl, but he was fast becoming Americanized. He dropped his difficult-to-pronounce Slavic name, Trsič, and signed his marriage register as Frank Miller. His brothers also took the surname Miller. Soon the three enterprising brothers were established as businessmen and property owners. Frank found a partner and opened the Mountain View Saloon under the name of Frank Miller & Co.

In 1894 he became an American citizen. He swore to uphold the Constitution and pledged to "entirely renounce and abjure all allegiance and fidelity to every foreign Prince, Potentate, State or Sovereignty whatever, and particularly to Francis Joseph, Emperor of Austria."

Life was going well for him, but Frank Miller hungered to make the fortune that tales of America had promised. In such a state of mind it was inevitable that he would catch the new "gold fever" that was sweeping the country.

Gold, in quantities never found anywhere in the world before, was discovered in the Klondike, Canada, in 1896. There was a stampede. By 1897 gold seekers had blazed a short, though difficult and dangerous, route to the Klondike goldfields from the port of Skagway and through Dyea on Alaska's southeastern coast. Landing by boat, carrying all their supplies on their backs, men and women by the thousands climbed over the steep Coast Mountains on the Chilkoot Trail to Canada. Many never made it to the Klondike, and most were too late to stake claims.

But a few became millionaires. The press went wild with stories of fabulous fortunes found in the Klondike. Jack London, the famous author who wrote *Call of the Wild*, made the journey himself. His stories of the North inspired many an adventurer.

Then in 1898, two years after the Klondike strike, gold was discovered at Nome, Alaska, an unimaginably distant spot on the coast of the Bering Sea. Three Scandanavian immigrants, two Swedes and a Norwegian, stumbled on the find. None of them knew much about gold prospecting. They were all laborers who had been through hard times. With nothing to lose, they headed north hoping to find their fortunes. And they did. After only a couple of months searching for gold, they staked their claims on one of the richest gold-bearing streams in Alaska.

As soon as word of the discovery was out, miners from the Yukon and other parts of Alaska rushed to Nome. Resentment against the three Scandinavian greenhorns rose. Not only were they newcomers to prospecting, but they were immigrants. And other immigrants were pouring into the new settlement. A rumor spread that aliens were conspiring to cheat "real" American miners out of their natural heritage.

It did not matter that the immigrants were naturalized American citizens. An ugly period of claim jumping began. Claims staked with foreign-sounding names—those ending in "son" or "berg" or with three consonants in a row like Trsič— were challenged as illegal by jealous men driven by greed. Nome nearly flared into a state of lawless violence. The U.S. Army prohibited the miners from carrying guns of any kind, but the situation was dangerous.

Then a strange and marvelous thing occurred. Someone on the beach looked down at his feet and noticed gold lying like seashells in the sand. The beach of Nome was rich with gold! Anyone could dig for it. No claims were needed.

All a person needed to mine on the beach was a shovel, a bucket or tin can to carry water in, and a rocker. A rocker, or cradle, was a crude wooden contraption, more efficient than a gold pan, used to separate the gold from the sand. Almost anyone with a hammer and some scraps of wood could make a rocker. One person shoveled the heavy wet sand into the hopper at the top of the rocker. Another poured water over the sand, while the third vigorously rocked the rocker to make the sand wash down through a blanket or canvas screen. Sand is lighter than gold, and while the sand washed through, the heavier flakes of gold were caught on the screen.

Soon the beach at Nome was jammed by people shoulder to shoulder shoveling wet black sand. Boatloads of fortune seekers braved the treacherous voyage from Seattle up the coasts of Canada and Alaska, through a dangerous pass in the Aleutian Islands and into the Bering Sea. Miners called the Nome beach a "poor man's paradise."

When he heard how easy it was to just step off the boat and start panning gold on the beach, Frank's gold fever overcame him. He joined the rush to Nome.

By the fall of 1899, Nome was bursting with close to 5,000 people in flimsy, wooden-frame buildings and over 500 tents. The largest tent in the city was a saloon. Frank had not sold his saloon in Anaconda, and he noted that there were more saloons than any other businesses in Nome. Harsh conditions led to heavy drinking.

Selling beer and whiskey to weary miners was cleaner and less backbreaking work than shoveling muck and sand in the cold winds off the Bering Sea. But competition for business lots was bitter and it was clear that the winter of 1899–1900 was going to be hard. Sanitation was almost impossible on the soggy tundra where nothing could be buried in the permanently frozen subsoil. Garbage and sewage were piling up. Typhoid fever, pneumonia, and bloody dysentery were spreading through the city.

Frank returned to Anaconda, Montana, without the hoped-for fortune in his pocket. But his saloon and roominghouse for single men was prospering. Annie, his wife, cooked pork chops, noodles, cabbage, and other traditional Slovene dishes for the smelter workers who rented their rooms. But news of more gold discoveries in Alaska kept Frank in a turmoil and fed his dreams of adventure. In 1901 a gold nugget seven inches long, four inches wide, and two inches thick, the largest ever found in Alaska, was discovered near Nome.

Then, in 1903, Frank's wife and helpmate, Annie, died. He was left with a small son and daughter and no mother to take care of them. Fortunately for Frank, his brother's wife had a sister who had just arrived from Ribnica, a village close to Ljubljana, the capital city of the Slovenes.

Mary Merhar was a striking young woman with smooth skin and dark hair. She was twenty-two, just the same age as Frank had been when he came to America. Without knowing a word of English, Mary left Austria in April, 1903, and traveled alone a full month before she reached Anaconda at the end of May. To her great joy when she joined her sister Angela in Anaconda, she found a whole community of her countrymen with whom she could talk.

Before long Mary lost her heart to Frank's two motherless children, Rosie and Eddy. Her sister and friends quickly pointed out to Mary that their father would make a good husband. Frank was clever and hardworking. Already he spoke English well enough to be a successful businessman and he owned the large wooden building that was his prosperous roominghouse and saloon. Success like this was not possible back in the villages they had come from. Within six months Mary and Frank were married. Mary, as industrious as her husband, cooked and cleaned for the roomers, just like Annie had. She also took care of the children, who soon included two little girls of their own.

Mary's dream of a better life seemed to be coming true. She was happy to have her own family and to live just down the street from her favorite sister in a community of other Slovenes. There were enough of them to keep the traditions of their culture and observe the holidays of the Catholic Church with all the feasts and celebrations that she was used to.

Then in 1902 Felix Pedro, an Italian immigrant, struck gold in the remote interior of Alaska. His discovery changed forever the lives of Frank and Mary Miller.

Few white men had ventured as far as Pedro into the heart of this enormous wilderness, and only a few Athapaskan Indians hunted and fished up and down its rivers. But when word got out, in 1903, that Pedro had made a strike, it started a gold rush into the Tanana Valley. A tent city sprang up near the confluence of the Tanana and Chena rivers in the center of Alaska. This mining camp was just 130 miles south of the Arctic Circle. It was named Fairbanks.

In the next few years, more gold was found in the surrounding Tanana hills. Three of Frank's bachelor friends staked claims on Pedro Creek and sent him word that he should join them.

Frank, although he was over forty and well established in business, was still ripe for adventure. He had savored the excitement of the gold rush at Nome. And he was incurably infected with the romance of Alaska. It was a territory where a man could be free of rules and regulations. There were no company towns run by big businesses like the Anaconda Mining Company. Frank wanted to go back to Alaska. Mary did not want to leave Anaconda. They argued. She cried. But gold, the magic word, pulled Frank once more into an unknown world, and Mary, with the four children, had to follow.

In the summer of 1906 Frank sold his Mountain View Saloon and roominghouse. Mary said good-bye to her beloved sister Angela, her last family tie.

It was early August and hot. Frank and Mary, with their four children, Rosie, Eddy, little Mary, and baby Albina, took the train from Montana to the northwest seaport of Seattle. In Seattle they bought supplies, then boarded a steamship for Alaska.

Mary's bad memories of her rough voyage across the Atlantic Ocean made her frightened of water. She was glad that land was in sight most of the trip up the Inside Passage. But the thick dark forests coming down to the water's edge looked gloomy and forbidding. And she had never seen such fog. It settled down silently, blotting out first the sky, then the water. The horizon disappeared and they sailed through an all-enveloping cold, clammy grayness.

But the sun shone at Skagway, Alaska, when, four days later, they boarded the narrow-gauge White Pass and Yukon Route Railroad to take them over the Coast Mountains. Little Rosie and Eddy pressed their noses against the train windows, excited and thrilled to be climbing up the mountain. But Mary sat rigid with fear. She held little Mary's hand tightly and cradled Albina in her arm. The White Pass and Yukon Route Railroad climbed 2,885 feet in only twenty miles up one of the steepest railroad grades in North America. The little train creaked and swayed as it chugged up the mountainside along cuts of jagged black rock. They were so close Mary thought the cliffs might tumble down on them. Branches of trees scraped the windows as they passed.

On the other side of the mountain, they crossed into Canada and came down, at the end of the day, into the bustling town of Whitehorse in the Yukon. There, near the headwaters of the mighty Yukon River, they clambered onto a flat-bottom, stern-wheeler riverboat to carry them into Alaska with all their bulky supplies: food, heavy winter clothing, diapers, bedding, shovels, saws, axes, Mary's trunk with her trousseau that she had sewed in her village in Austria, and the two rolled-up mattresses that she had bought in Seattle.

Now Mary was excited. The riverboat had a handsome lounge, a dining room with white tablecloths, and staterooms with polished mahogany railings around the bunks and counter tops. It was much smaller than the steamship from Seattle, and a river was not as scary as an ocean. So she relaxed and decided to enjoy herself.

Mary was twenty-five and it was her last chance for a few days without cooking, cleaning, and washing before she faced the backbreaking work of building a new life in Alaska. Even though she knew Frank would be furious if he caught her, she recklessly tossed the babies' dirty diapers out of her cabin porthole as they steamed across Lake Bennett and down the Yukon River. Covering her mouth with the back of her hand, Mary giggled and felt deliciously wicked.

But the deeper they traveled into the Yukon wilderness the more overpowering the immense silence became. The river ran silent and cold. Scarcely a bird cried. A tremendous sense of the vastness and isolation of the country they were coming into weighed down on Mary. Frank paced the decks and said little except when he shouted at her to keep the children quiet.

Occasionally they stopped at woodcutters' camps to take on

wood from the huge neat stacks of 4x4x8 logs for the boat's furnace that powered the stern paddle-wheel. Every day they passed battered wrecks of riverboats or rafts from the Klondike gold rush days beached on rocks and sandbars.

After nearly three hundred miles through canyons, steep banks and a few small rapids, the White River entered the Yukon, widening it to nearly double its size. Then the stern-wheeler rounded a bend where another great river, the Pelly, joins the Yukon. There on a high bluff the passengers saw the small settlement of Fort Selkirk, a trading post where Athapaskan Indians and white trappers brought their furs. Eagerly Mary and Frank went ashore, Mary carrying the baby with little Mary, Eddy, and Rosie trailing behind.

As they followed their fellow passengers to the large log trading post, Mary spied a little log church behind the cluster of cabins. Dropping back to investigate, she hesitantly pushed open the rough-hewn door and slipped inside. In this simple church, Mary Merhar Miller dropped to her knees in front of the blue-robed Virgin Mary. She crossed herself and gave thanks that she and her family had made their journey safely thus far and that here, like a miracle in the wilderness, she had found a Catholic church. For Mary, this little log church was a life-sustaining link with all that she had had to leave behind.

After only a few hours the stern-wheeler continued its journey, another two hundred miles down the Yukon to Dawson City, Canada. There Mary and Frank and other passengers had to wait nine days for an even smaller steamer to take them nearly a thousand miles farther into Alaska.

Now the wider, shallower, silt-filled Yukon River became a maze choked with islands and treacherous sandbars. It ran north to Fort Yukon on the Arctic Circle, then bent southwest flowing across the wide Yukon Flats toward the Bering Sea. Several times curious black bears peering from the scrub forests were spotted by passengers on deck. Moose were seen crashing away from the noise of the small stern-wheeler.

At the tiny trading settlement of Tanana the steamer left the Yukon and turned southeast up the Tanana River and into the Chena River to Fairbanks. It was the last boat on the river before the winter ice closed navigation. On September 27, 1906, nearly two months after they left Anaconda, Frank and Mary Miller arrived in Fairbanks, Alaska. Frank was excited and anxious to find his mining friends. But Mary took one look at the town and her heart sank.

A year earlier Fairbanks had been almost destroyed by a flood. Then in May, 1906, a devastating fire swept through the main part of town. The wooden buildings, packed with sawdust insulation, flared up like matchboxes. In forty minutes the whole business section burned to the ground. Everyone began working feverishly cutting and hauling trees to rebuild the town before winter set in. Goods that were saved from the burning stores were stashed in every available cabin.

Frank's friends had written to him that he would have no trouble renting a cabin to live in once he got to Fairbanks. But all Frank could find was a one-room, sod-roofed cabin made of green logs for his family's first winter in Alaska.

It was also too late in the season for Frank to do any mining. But he was charged with energy and bursting for action. Fairbanks was booming in spite of the fire. Merchants were scrambling to serve a population that had grown from 800 in 1903 to 10,000 in 1906.

Fairbanks had boasted that it was "the largest log cabin town in the world." Now it was the largest and fastest-growing city in Alaska, with three banks, three churches, two daily newspapers, several large sawmills, a score of saloons, and hundreds of log cabins spreading fanlike out from the central business section on the river.

Everyone had a get-rich-quick outlook and Frank began scouting for ways to make money immediately. Settling on the business he knew best, Frank bought the Miner's Home Saloon that advertised "Pool tables and Rooms," to support his family until he made his fortune in gold mining.

That first winter Mary and Frank experienced cold and darkness such as they had never known before. In the dead of winter there were only three hours of daylight. Temperatures dropped from forty to sixty degrees below zero. The foggy air became so cold it burned the skin. Mary kept the children inside the small cabin.

But there were beautiful days, too, when the sun shone brightly, the air was still and dry, and the snow sparkled. Then Frank went with the men into the woods to cut trees, load them on horse-drawn sleds, and bring them home to saw and split into stove lengths to heat his cabin and the Miner's Home.

When spring came, the ice melted and the Chena River flooded Fairbanks again, though not as badly as in 1905. Water inched up the walls of cabins close to the river. Frank had to borrow a rowboat to ferry Mary and the children to higher ground. No more winters in *that* cabin, she declared. Or springs! When the water went down, tiny mice popped up through the tree poles that made up the floors.

So that summer Frank and several of his Slovene friends built a larger, sturdier log cabin on Garden Island, across the river on higher ground near his Miner's Home Saloon. When Mary moved in she opened the trunk she had carried her trousseau in all the way from Ribnica to Montana to Alaska. It was filled with hand-embroidered sheets, pillowcases, petticoats, and linens. Now she found that every piece was ruined by mildew. The green logs of the cramped cabin in which they had spent the winter had exuded dampness. Mary sat down on a tree stump and cried.

Their new cabin was better built. Frank chinked the spaces between the round unpeeled logs with newspapers and moss and cemented them over to keep out the drafts. He used lumber for the rafters and bought tin for the roofing.

The cabin had a living room, two bedrooms, the larger one for the children and the smaller for Mary and Frank, and a kitchen with a hand pump for water in the summer when the ground was not frozen. In winter the iron stove Mary cooked on heated the cabin. At the back of the stove she kept pans filled with snow to melt for water. The toilet was an outhouse behind the cabin. In the next twelve years Mary and Frank had seven more children, all born in their log cabin home.

All this time Frank was looking for gold. In 1908 there was a strike on the Iditarod River west of Fairbanks and north of the Kuskokwim Mountains. The next summer Frank went to the Iditarod. He staked a mining claim, opened a Miner's Home, and returned to Fairbanks. By the summer of 1910 about 2,500 people from all over Alaska and the lower 48 states converged on the Iditarod district.

In those early days there was little machinery in Alaska and it was difficult to work a mine when pay dirt or veins of gold were from 10 to 200 feet deep in the permafrost as they often were in the interior. Most of Alaska's ground is permanently frozen just a few inches or a few feet under the thin topsoil. This frozen ground is called permafrost.

Because of the permafrost, gold mining was tedious and often dangerous work. Boilers fueled by wood were needed to heat water. The hot water was shot through hoses with firemen's nozzles to thaw the ground. Mine shafts had to be dug with picks and shovels. Men were lowered to dig tunnels along the veins of pay dirt. The frozen gold-bearing dirt first had to be thawed, then cut out of the ground, and hauled to the surface in buckets. There it was run through sluice boxes to wash out the gold.

Many of the miners in the Iditarod were from Fairbanks, where the gold boom had peaked. By 1910 more than $30 million had been mined from three creeks near the town: Cleary, Ester, and Fairbanks. Several lucky men who had staked their claims in the right spots were millionaires. But the best gold-bearing land had been mined.

People began to move on, until by 1915 Fairbanks had lost nearly two-thirds of its population. Businesses failed, cabins stood empty, and the riverboats leaving Fairbanks were jammed. Only 3,500 people remained in this once-booming town of 10,000.

Mary would gladly have left too, but Frank decided they would stay on. Nobody would buy his hotels and saloons and he had invested too much in his businesses and gold claims to walk away from them. Besides, he liked the country. He liked the action, the openness, and the freewheeling ways of doing business. He had faith in its future. And he was building a reputation as a successful businessman and a generous partner in mining ventures. Anyone who had a good prospect he was willing to stake.

Frank's mining interests expanded beyond the Kuskokwim to the Livengood, Bonnefield, and Chena Hot Springs districts. In the summers he hired men and worked with them at his mines, always cleaning up enough gold to keep him looking for that big strike. But the Miner's Home, and the other Miner's Home he opened in the gold-rush town of Iditarod, proved to be more lucrative than all the gold mines Frank Miller ever staked.

During the summer while Frank was away managing his

mines, Mary collected the bills and kept the books for the Miner's Home saloons. Soon she began to tuck $20 gold pieces into her apron pockets. Back in her cabin, she slid the shiny gold pieces into her cedar chest under her clothes. It was gold for her dream: to send her children to college.

With a heartfelt sense of how hard it was for other immigrant women who had no family or friends when they arrived in Fairbanks, Mary went to visit them. Men outnumbered women by at least five to one. Often the women Mary visited were "mail order brides" whose families or village priests in Europe had arranged their marriages to miners they thought were millionaires in Alaska.

Even when Mary could not understand their language she knew how much it meant to these young, bewildered, homesick brides to see another woman. Their "millionaire" husbands had nothing more than log cabins and hard work to offer them when they arrived on this northern frontier. Years later these women remembered gratefully how Mary Miller came when they had their babies. She would sit on a chair near their beds with a calm, comforting look on her face, her back very straight, and her hands folded in her lap "like a lady."

To feed their growing family, Mary and Frank farmed, first on land behind their cabin and then on a 160-acre homestead they acquired west of Fairbanks. They were no longer primarily gold seekers; they had become pioneer settlers. They raised goats for milk and pigs to slaughter for sausages, chops, and head cheese. In the long hours of summer sunlight their cabbages grew to enormous sizes and they made sauerkraut in big wooden barrels. Frank bought a horse, which had been brought up the Yukon on a stern-wheeler, to pull a plow, and they planted potatoes, turnips, beets, rhubarb, and carrots.

All the farm skills Mary and Frank had learned growing up

in their villages in Austria served them well in the remote interior of Alaska. They knew how to grow and prepare enough food to last through the long isolation of winter when no supplies could be brought in. The last shipment with goods for Fairbanks left Seattle about August 20 on a steamship that delivered it to a stern-wheeler at the mouth of the Yukon River on the Bering Sea. Then, at the beginning of September, the stern-wheeler had to make the 1,200-mile journey upriver and return before freeze-up. The spring shipment, with fresh eggs, lemons and oranges, arrived about the third week in May.

But the growing Miller family ate well during those eight winter months. They had a natural deep freeze for meats and vegetables they raised. The moose or caribou Frank shot in the fall and cut into roasts, chops, and steaks was frozen solid in the cache behind the house. When Mary baked bread, she put the loaves on the windowsill. There they froze instantly and she could bring in a loaf at a time as needed.

As soon as the children were old enough to hold a hoe they were put to work in the garden, cultivating, weeding, and watering. They picked wild cranberries and blueberries, dug potatoes, fed the pigs, and herded the goats. Frank drove the family to work at a feverish pitch in the long sunlight hours of the short summer. It was a race to be ready for winter. Survival depended on their own efforts. No one could afford to be idle.

The gold boom was over, dreams of great wealth began to fade, and Frank became a harsh father in a harsh land. Mary had her ninth and last baby, named Billy, in 1919. In 1920 the population of Fairbanks had dwindled down to 1,155 and all of Alaska was in a slump.

Then in 1923 the government-owned railroad that had been started in 1915 from the seaport town of Seward reached Fairbanks. It enabled large mining companies to bring in huge

Frank and Mary Miller's wedding portraits, October 18, 1903.

Keystone View Company, copyright, 1898, by B. L. Singley.

Prospectors bound for the Klondike goldfields, Chilkoot Pass, Alaska, 1898.

Fairbanks, around 1920.

The Millers' new house, around 1935.

Frank and Mary Miller and children, Billy, Josephine, Bobby, Albina, and Emma, 1920.

Mary Miller, Queen of the Fairbanks
Winter Ice Festival, 1936.

Jim Dodson

Millie Dodson, 1937

After the crash of the *Sea Pigeon*, Jim took to the woods to recuperate and regain his strength, late summer, 1931.

Jim Dodson by his Stinson Reliant, late 1930s.

Jim and Millie Dodson, 1940.

Willie Hensley,
Kotzebue, around 1952.

With shee fish,
May, 1956.

Willie and friends
fishing, 1968.

Willie Hensley in Yakutya,
mid-Siberia, 1977.

Receiving the Gold Pan Award,
1980, for the outstanding individual of the year from the Anchorage Chamber of Commerce.

dredges and modern equipment to work the ground the early miners had skimmed with their primitive methods. The Alaska Railroad saved Fairbanks.

President Warren Harding, the first U.S. president to visit Alaska, came to Fairbanks to drive in the golden railroad spike at its terminus near Frank Miller's Miner's Home Saloon. There was a great celebration. President Harding patted Billy's head and foresaw a great future for Alaska.

A group of hard-drinking White House reporters whooped it up at the Miner's Home Saloon. When they left, they took with them the seven-foot-tall Alaskan black spruce figure that stood in front of Frank's saloon like a cigar-store Indian. The reporters dressed the wooden figure in a bandanna and bonnet and dubbed it Princess Alice after the late President Teddy Roosevelt's daughter, Alice Roosevelt Longworth.

The White House reporters carried "Princess Alice" all the way back to Washington, D.C. There it was adopted as the mascot for the National Press Club, the most prestigious organization of journalists in the country. "Princess Alice" now stands on a pedestal, guarding the entrance to the president's office in the National Press Club building. A plaque explains how she came from the Miner's Home Saloon in the heart of Alaska to the heart of Washington, D.C., a rustic legacy from the last frontier.

When the Alaska Railroad acquired the land where the Miner's Home Saloon stood to build a fine new depot, Frank used the logs of his dismantled building to construct, opposite the railroad depot, one of the largest homes in Fairbanks. In 1924 the Miller family moved from their two-bedroom cabin into the spacious new log house that was two-and-a-half stories high.

The house had an ornate front door and a big back porch with a second-story porch above it edged by a spindle railing.

Most impressive of all, it had a broad veranda that wrapped around two sides of the house with square, finished porch columns and newel posts. Frank and Mary Miller were successful pioneers proudly taking their place among the first families of Fairbanks.

In their first twenty years in the Territory, when Alaska was a raw wilderness, Mary and Frank had accomplished miracles. As twentieth-century pioneers in the north, they had faced frontier hardships as severe as those faced by the nineteenth-century pioneers of America's West. And, like many of the West's pioneers, gold lured them but the land kept them. But in one important way Alaska's pioneers were different.

Because the country they settled was so enormous and difficult to survive in and there were so few people, each Alaskan was highly valued. In their isolation, Alaskan pioneers depended on each other for survival. Theirs was a new and classless society. In the tightly knit community of Fairbanks, Mary and Frank Miller were able to achieve a status equal to their considerable abilities. In one great leap from their villages in Europe they built a new life in a new land. In one generation they discarded their ethnic identity to become, first Americans and then, Alaskans.

The eleven children they raised were true Alaskans. They grew up independent, frugal, resilient, and physically hardened by manual labor. And Mary Miller achieved her dearest dream. Dipping into her hidden gold, Mary sent her children, one by one, both daughters and sons, to college—an extraordinary accomplishment for those times.

Frank's faith in the future of the Alaskan frontier was justified by his children. In the expanding Territory they found a wealth of opportunities that he and Mary could never have dreamed of. Some established their own businesses. Albina became a Lieutenant-Commander in the United States Navy.

Henry went to the Naval Academy at Annapolis and became Alaska's first Rear Admiral. With the last of her gold cache, Mary sent her baby, Billy, to a prep school in San Francisco, and he became a U.S. Foreign Service officer with Fairbanks as his home base. They were pioneer children all, stubborn optimists, who believed that in America hard work and perseverance could overcome any obstacles. Their parents' lives had proved it.

The last great gold strike in Alaska was in Livengood in 1914. Gold mining, as Frank Miller had discovered, was part of the boom-and-bust cycles in Alaska's history. In a later boom in 1974, gold prices shot up after the government lifted restrictions on the sale of gold in the United States. But large machines now overshadowed the individual miner in Alaska. The world's largest oceangoing mineral dredge, fourteen stories high, worked the seabed for gold off the coast of Nome, site of the fabled turn-of-the-century strike that had first drawn Frank Miller to Alaska.

In the 1980s the mining business in sand, gravel, and stone for construction was more profitable than gold production. Gold is still an important subsidiary part of the Alaska economy. But, in the last third of the twentieth century, the oil industry dominated the state as Alaska's prime source of wealth. And a new breed of fortune seekers, who would not stay, flocked north to the fields of "black gold."

JIM & MILLIE DODSON:
Pioneers of the Skies

"If a man has any greatness in him,
it comes to light, not in one flamboyant hour,
but in the ledger of his daily work."

Beryl Markham
West with the Night

In the winter of 1936 snow began to fall in August and now
it was early December. The mountains, hills, and marshes
were blanketed in a smooth covering of white. Daylight lasted
only a few hours but the arctic sun was bright. Jim Dodson,
a lone Alaska bush pilot, squinted to see out of the cockpit of
his small plane. The sun's slanting rays reflecting on the snow
made the world below him dazzling white. Ice had grown from
the banks of lakes, rivers, and streams, met in the middle and
become solid. The ice sealed over the dark lines and large
mirrors of water, hiding these landmarks in the frozen bril-
liance of the white landscape. Flying low, at about 1,000 feet,
Jim strained to see faint shadows that would indicate the
rounding contours of hills and indentations of rivers.

This area, north of the Arctic Circle and the Yukon Flats,

was, like most of Alaska, still unmapped in the 1930s. There were no roads here. No survey teams had charted the rivers or climbed the hills to triangulate and measure the mountains. But Jim carried his own map in his mind's eye. He had made and memorized it on countless flights from Fort Yukon up the great rivers that fed into the mighty Yukon River: the Black, the Porcupine, the Coleen, the Sheenjek, the Christian, and the Chandalar. He learned the way each river flowed, its great loops and where it narrowed through the hills and canyons, and where each cabin or little village sat along its banks. In winter he could detect the slight depressions in the snow that marked dogsled trails which were lifelines to follow if his engine began to fail or snow-filled clouds closed in around him.

Jim's plane was a single-engine, single-winged, fabric-covered, four-seat Stinson Reliant Gullwing. Its top speed was 130 miles per hour and its cruising range 500 miles. There was a small luggage compartment in the fuselage, but he had taken out the two rear seats so he would have additional room to stack cargo in the cabin. In this monoplane, only 27 feet long, he carried supplies to the few lone trappers on the rivers who spent their winters trapping beaver, ermine, muskrats, mink, otter, fox, and wolves. In the summers he carried miners with their equipment who worked the soil for gold.

Whenever he flew, Jim studied the earth below him, memorizing its shape so he would know it in every season. He was flying beyond the reach of radio over a vast and empty land.

On this brilliant winter day, Jim had flown up the East Fork Chandalar River at the foot of the Brooks Range to deliver supplies to a trapper. In the fall he had taken the wheels off his plane and put on skis so he could land on the snow. It was a routine flight. Heading back to Fort Yukon, he watched for any sign of life in the trackless wilderness—perhaps a lone wolf or a moose. But the landscape was void, silent, and closed in the lock of winter.

In the late fall this barren land had been covered with thousands of caribou heading south from the shores of the Arctic Ocean across the Porcupine River to their winter range in the Ogilvie Mountains of Canada. Over 170,000 caribou make up the great Porcupine herd. Jim had seen them many times, their dark shapes outlined on the white ground. The caribou traveled their ancient route south in lines that were miles long. Athapaskan Indians at Arctic Village and Old Crow and other settlements along the caribou route counted on these migrating caribou to supply them with food for the winter.

Then suddenly, glancing out of the corner of his eye, past the wing strut, Jim thought he saw some dark spots move on the white ground below. It was too late in the season to see caribou. He banked and circled back. Flying lower, Jim saw that it was a dog team and two men. They were in the middle of a frozen lake. The tracks behind them zigzagged across the ice. But they seemed to have stopped moving. The dogs were lying down.

Jim made two low circles over them. Neither of the men waved. Jim looked for a place to land. The lake was smooth and he was able to taxi his small Stinson up to the strange little group of men and dogs.

Jim jumped down out of his plane and ran to them. The two men's faces were nearly covered by their fur-edged parkas but he saw that they were young Athapaskan Indians. They could scarcely stand. When they saw Jim, they nodded their heads. But they did not speak. Then one of the men collapsed onto the sled.

Jim raced back to his plane. He threw out the trappers' bundles of furs onto the frozen lake as fast as he could to make room for the men. Then he unhitched the dogs from the sled and dragged it with the young man who had collapsed over to the plane. He heaved and shoved him into the cabin. Hurrying back to the other Indian, he took his arm and led him to the plane.

The sun was sinking behind the horizon. There was barely enough daylight time left to get to Fort Yukon. And there was no room for the dogs in the small plane. They had to be left on the lake beside the stack of furs that Jim would come back for later. Jim knew the exhausted dogs could not survive long enough for someone to come for them. They would freeze and the wolves would find them, but he had no choice.

As they flew through the darkening sky, the Athapaskan in the seat beside Jim murmured. "Arctic Village—no caribou." In a flash Jim understood what he had suspected.

Somehow the caribou had altered their migration route south so that they did not pass Arctic Village as they had since time immemorial. Without the caribou there was no hunting and no meat. The tiny village of only forty people was starving. They had chosen two of their strongest young men to go by dogsled to Fort Yukon for help. But the men were already too weak from lack of food to make the long, cold journey. Jim had spotted them when they could go no farther.

Traders and storekeepers in Fort Yukon rallied to aid the people of Arctic Village. The next day and for several days afterward Jim flew food supplies into the remote village. He found that the villagers had already killed and eaten most of their sled dogs and that their meager food supplies were nearly gone. Some of the older people already had died of starvation.

Jim and no one in Fort Yukon expected to be paid for the emergency supplies or fuel to fly them to Arctic Village. But, a couple of months later, in February, 1937, when Jim dropped by Harry Carter's Trading Post in Fort Yukon, he found a letter addressed to him: James Dodson, airplane man. It read,

"Dear Friend, I send $10 to you from Paul Tritt, Arctic Village, Alaska."

In the sparsely populated territory of Alaska, friendships were fast and a person's character was known up and down the rivers and in every village. Natives along the Porcupine and Yukon rivers who were children in the 1930s and '40s remembered in the 1980s and '90s how they grew up "playing Jim Dodson" and how Jim gave them their first airplane rides.

"Bush pilots were gods to us," said Mary Jane Fate, an Athapaskan Indian who became the first president of her Native village corporation which received land and money benefits under the 1971 Alaska Native Claims Settlement Act. Mary Jane's village is Rampart on the Yukon River. When she was growing up, she traveled with her parents as they hunted and fished in the traditional Native subsistence way of life. Rampart was their base and a frequent stop for the Jim Dodson Air Service. She remembers how the sound of Jim's plane sent a thrill through the children at Rampart. "He was our link to the outside world," she said. "Jim helped us and explained things. We would imitate the way he walked, everything he did. If he was too busy to smile, we were in agony until he came back. Jim never looked down on us."

The entire population of Alaska—Indian, Eskimo, Aleut, and white—in the 1930s was only 65,000, less than a small city in the States. So every person made a difference, everything he did was known—who could be trusted, who could not, who was good at what, and who was generous and who was not. In this atmosphere, Jim Dodson built a reputation for fairness, generosity, and rock-bottom reliability. He epitomized the spirit of rugged, frontier individualism tempered by a sense of community responsibility.

Jim was a pioneer, like those in the western movement of the United States, who carved out a new land by clearing, ploughing, and planting fields. Except he was pioneering air routes in the sky rather than roads through the wilderness. Like all of the early Alaska Bush pilots, Jim was a unique pioneer in a unique land.

The first glimpse Jim had of Alaska was from the deck of a boat. It was the summer of 1921 and he felt lucky to have landed a summer job on a cannery tender (a boat that transports catches of fish from other boats to the cannery on shore). As the tender sailed north from Seattle to Bristol Bay, Jim was filled with a sense of adventure. They steamed past shores dark with evergreen forests and mountains rising straight from the water. He was stirred by the grandeur and beauty of such an immense, unspoiled land. In every port there was excited talk about the opportunities in Alaska.

Fishing, mining, and trapping were still the main industries. But now, aviation held the promise of greater efficiency and more profits for miners and trappers. Alaska was too large and the terrain too rugged for any but limited road building. By plane, a trip into the interior of the territory could be made in hours that had required days or weeks of rigorous travel by the older methods of riverboats or dogsleds.

If they flew, miners would not lose precious time out of the short three-month summer season waiting until the ice broke up and cleared out of the rivers to get to their mines by riverboats. And they would not have to leave their mines before freeze-up, about mid-September, when the rivers were still navigable. Trappers found that their dogs were good airplane passengers. They could fly them with their bundles of dried fish, the dogs' staple food, to the trapping sites at the beginning of winter. Then they could work their traplines right up to the last of the season without worrying about leaving early in the spring when there was still enough snow on the ground to run their sleds back to town.

Jim understood that airplanes were the only means by which this huge territory would ever become accessible. And he knew that now was the time for pioneering pilots in Alaska. He was determined to become one. But he didn't know how to fly and he had no money.

But he had a plan. After graduating from the University of Washington, Jim joined the Naval Reserve to learn to fly. By 1929 he was on active duty in the Navy, assigned as a pilot to the U.S.S. *Langley*, the world's first aircraft carrier. In the Navy's rigorous training program Jim learned to navigate and to bring his open cockpit plane down on the short, limited space of an aircraft carrier deck, or if he were flying with pontoons, to land on water. These were skills he knew would serve him well in the Alaskan Bush, where there were no air routes or landing fields. There he would have to chart his own course and search for small strips of ground in the lumpy tundra or for gravel bars in the rivers level enough to land on.

The next year, 1930, Jim felt ready to embark on his great adventure. The year 1929 had seen the great stock market crash, when businesses collapsed and banks failed all across the United States. Most stocks and bonds were worthless and people feared that their money would continue to lose its value. Gold seemed the only sound investment. Gold prices shot up and Alaska boomed. Prospectors hurried north. As the ranks of jobless in the States swelled and an economic depression settled in, the only Promised Land left seemed to be the Territory of Alaska.

Pilots flocked into the country, some by boat hoping to find a job flying someone else's airplane, some with their own planes, dismantled, crated, and shipped north because there were not enough landing fields between Seattle and Alaska to fly there.

Jim, with only his Navy pay in his pocket, booked passage

on the Alaska Steamship line as far as Ketchikan, the first stop over the Canadian border in southeast Alaska. His real capital was his Navy credentials, more solid than those of most pilots who had learned to fly after a few lessons and whose only experience was barnstorming in the States. Jim's other asset was his top physical condition: broad-shouldered, lean and muscular, he was a handsome young man with a confident manner and a friendly twinkle in his blue eyes.

When he stepped off the boat, Jim learned that there were only three airplanes in Ketchikan. Two of them, Stinson pontoon monoplanes, named the *Northbird* and the *Sea Pigeon*, were owned by Pioneer Airways of Alaska. He applied to Pioneer Airways and was hired to fly them.

In the early days of flying, when pilots did not have elaborate instrument boards and beacons and radio contact to guide them, they had to rely on their own keen eyesight, good reflexes, and quick sensory reactions. Those who had "the touch" sensed without looking what their few instruments told them: their speed, height, whether they were flying level and in which direction. These were indicated on their airspeed, altimeter, bank and turn indicator, and compass. Often those basic instruments gave false readings, so pilots learned to trust their senses. Close observation and experience sharpened their intuitive sense of how weather would develop. When they were caught in darkness or weather closed in and they lost visual contact with the ground, they flew "blind," relying more on their acute sensibilities than on instruments that could read wrong or fail.

Jim had "the touch." Flying exhilarated him. It challenged him intellectually and physically. He learned that when he had to fly above a ground fog that water showed darker than the land beneath the fog, so he could follow the coastal shoreline. He skimmed up inlets, through passes between the mountains, and over countless unnamed lakes. He flew on crystal-clear days when the snow-covered Coast Mountains were shining white against a bright blue sky and sunlight sparkled on the inlet waters. And he flew through sudden squalls, in rainstorms, and in windstorms. Alaska was where he wanted to be. Pioneer Airways sent him on trip after trip.

A mother, who claimed her twelve-day-old child to be the youngest-ever passenger in an airplane, was quoted in the local newspaper: "Our daughter slept soundly at an elevation of 3,000 feet over Prince of Wales Island. The trip, which would have taken twenty-four hours by boat, took exactly forty-one minutes in the *Northbird* of Pioneer Airways, piloted by Jim Dodson." Jim's reputation as a skilled pilot with sound judgment was growing rapidly.

Then, on May 3, 1931, Jim Dodson crashed.

He was taking off in the *Sea Pigeon* from Salmon Lake, north of Ketchikan. Suddenly his plane went into a spin. He didn't have enough altitude to bring it out of the spin. In a sickening flash he knew it would crash.

When Jim regained consciousness blood was pouring from his broken nose. His right leg was smashed. The passenger beside him was unconscious. The two men in the back seats were badly hurt.

Fighting pain, Jim eased himself out of the cockpit and clung to the wing. He saw that they were on a lonely little island close to the lake's shore. He realized he would have to splint his fractured leg in order to stand up. Reaching back into the plane he pulled a small axe from his emergency pack and chopped up the wooden wing to make splints. Struggling to keep from passing out with pain, he tied the splints around his leg with cloth strips he tore from his shirt. Next he fashioned a small paddle. Then, dragging his splinted leg, he mustered all his strength to hack a pontoon off the plane.

Jim could not move the unconscious man. But with great effort he managed to maneuver the two other injured men onto the pontoon, straddle it, and paddle them to shore. He covered them with jackets and a tarp, making them as comfortable as he could. Then he told them to lie quietly. He would go for help.

Once more Jim straddled the pontoon. With his small, makeshift paddle he started down the long cold lake to look for help. He knew there was a cabin sometimes used by fishermen at the far end. His action was an incredible feat of physical strength and determination.

When Pioneer Airways found that the *Sea Pigeon* was overdue for its return to Ketchikan, they sent out a search plane. Jim heard the drone of the engine and, with a spurt of hope, waved his paddle high above his head. Finally the search plane sighted him far down Salmon Lake.

Before his passengers could be flown out from the crash site, one man died. Another had two broken legs, the third fractured thighs and shoulders. Jim was shipped to a hospital in Seattle. His nose had to be rebuilt. The doctor said his leg looked as if a sledgehammer had pounded it into hundreds of little fragments.

"Seattle Flyer Hero of Alaskan Crash" read the *Seattle Daily Times* front page story. Telegrams and letters poured into the hospital for Jim from friends and fellow fliers. "Folks up here are very proud of your courage and grit in carrying on the way you did after the crack-up," wrote a pilot from Juneau. "That takes the real stuff and you have it." "Admire your wonderful courage," wired another. "Hope to see you back on the run soon." But the medical opinion was that Jim would never fly again.

However, when the doctors made their diagnosis, they did not take into account Jim's determination. A series of operations and skin grafts left him with a rebuilt nose, a somewhat shorter and slightly stiff right leg. But, through painful exercises he devised, he managed to obtain enough mobility in his ankle to work the foot pedal that operates the rudder of a plane.

By April, 1932, just short of a year after his accident, Jim passed his flight physical examination. With his pilot's license reissued, Jim headed back to the land he loved. This time he went farther north, to the booming town of Anchorage, and there he met his life's partner. Her name was Millie Jones.

Millie and Jim met over a cup of hot chocolate at Sally's Sweet Shop in Anchorage where Millie was working as manager and waitress. Three months later, in March, 1935, they were married.

A slim, handsome, dark-haired young woman, Millie Jones had grown up in New England on a fox ranch. She came north with her family when her father decided to raise foxes at Kasilof on the Kenai Peninsula south of Anchorage. Like Jim, she was mentally and physically tough. They both enjoyed the sense of accomplishment achieved by hard work. But neither of them could have known then that they were forging a business as well as a marriage partnership.

Shortly after they were married, Jim got a job flying a plane owned by Fred Bowman, a mechanic, that was a sister ship to the *Spirit of St. Louis*, the plane in which Charles Lindbergh made his historic solo flight across the Atlantic in 1927. In Jim's log books were entries such as: "Feb. 18. Forced landing. Gas valve plugged. O.K."; "Nov. 10. Tried to go to Cache Creek on skis. No snow beyond Sustina."; "Nov. 13. Horsfeld to Jack Lake. Forced landing." Flying was just part of the job. Basic mechanics and general resourcefulness on the ground were a must for Alaskan Bush pilots.

When Millie and Jim's twin boys, Warren and Jimmy, Jr., were three months old, Jim entered a business arrangement with Dr. Bart Larue, a Bureau of Indian Affairs dentist. Dr. Larue needed a pilot to fly his Stinson Reliant Gullwing when he visited the far-flung villages of interior Alaska. He was based in Ruby, a small Indian village on the Yukon River. But he often stayed in other villages for as long as two months and during that time Jim could use the plane for his own commercial purposes.

In early March when the days were still short, the snow deep, and the wind whistling down the frozen Yukon sent temperatures plummeting to fifty or sixty degrees below zero, Jim, Millie, and the three-month-old twins moved to Ruby. Their new home was a two-room log cabin on the riverbank. Ruby had two trading posts that bought furs from the Athapaskan Indian trappers and carried supplies for the gold mines nearby. The trappers' dogsled trail ran past the cabin.

Jim helped settle his family and then left with the Stinson to find passengers and freight wherever he could. In the next three months he got back to Ruby only three times. Millie was alone with her baby boys.

There was no water in the cabin so Millie took a washtub into the backyard where the snow was deepest and easier to scoop into the tub. Then she sat down and dragged the tub up to her. She would sit and drag, sit and drag, inching her way to the cabin where she heaved the tub onto the stove to melt the snow. The water content of snow is very small, so Millie kept one tub on the stove constantly. Her stove, made from an oil drum, was called a "Yukon stove." Jim had left her a huge woodpile to keep the stove going night and day as it was the only source of heat. He had rigged a clothesline on a big pulley between two trees. Every day Millie washed fifty to one hundred diapers. She hung them on the line to freeze, which bleached them very white. Then she stacked the frozen diapers like cord wood and brought them in the cabin to thaw.

Finally spring came. By mid-April the frozen ground began to thaw and animals and insects began to stir. The logs of the cabin walls began to dry and contract and to pull away from the wooden floor. Hordes of tiny field mice scooted in through the cracks. Millie shrieked and grabbed her broom.

The thaw also brought mosquitoes so thick Millie could not go outside without a mosquito net over her face to keep from breathing them in. She tied nets over the clothes baskets Jimmy and Warren slept in. In minutes the nets were black with mosquitoes. She burned Buhach, a mosquito repellent, but its odiferous smoke barely kept the mosquitoes at bay. At night their buzzing was so loud it awakened her. To go out of the cabin to hang the diapers on the line, she wore coveralls with work gloves tied at her wrists, her pants legs tied over her shoepacs, and a big hat with a net covering her face and tied around her neck. The warmer wind dried the diapers on the line but the ice in the Yukon River still remained frozen.

Finally Jim returned to Ruby with the happy news that he could move them all to Fairbanks, the supply center for interior Alaska, a real town. He had a job flying for Wien Alaska Airlines.

Noel Wien was one of the great pioneers of Alaska aviation. In 1925 he was the first pilot to fly across and land above the Arctic Circle. He made the first commercial flight between Fairbanks and Nome. In 1929 he hauled furs from a ship which was frozen in the ice off North Cape, Siberia, thus setting the record of the first round trip by air between the two continents of America and Asia. The four Wien brothers were all involved in flying and Wien Alaska Airlines was a family enterprise.

Jim flew a year for the Wiens. By then he had saved enough

money to buy his own plane. His dream was coming true. In the local newspaper, *The Fairbanks Daily News Miner*, he placed an ad: "FLYING—Up or Down the Yukon and to the Kuskokwim—Call Jim Dodson."

Fairbanks, by the mid-1930s, had become the flying capital of interior Alaska. Planes were owner-operated, their comings and goings reported in the newspaper's "Aviation News" column which was read daily by everyone in Fairbanks. An April 30, 1937, entry read, "Harbingers of spring—the black bear coming out of his den and the wild gander winging northward—are reported by airman Jimmy Dodson. Flying across Lake Minchumina yesterday, Dodson observed three large flocks of geese, and on a hillside near the junction of the Chena and the Tanana rivers he circled a black bear that had just come out of his den to laze around in the sun."

On December 13, "Aviation News" reported, "Pilot Jim Dodson returned to Fairbanks this morning after a few days flying in the Fort Yukon district. From a camp on the Black River, about 100 miles from Fort Yukon, Dodson took Joe Carrol and a native boy to Fort Yukon yesterday. The lad could not speak English and his mother had sewed a sign on the back of his parka, 'Passenger for Fort Yukon.' "

December 22: "Two of the happiest young men in Fairbanks are Jimmy and Warren Dodson, each wearing a new parka of velvety reindeer calf with wolf trim. Their father, Pilot Jim Dodson, brought the warm parkas from Beaver. The twins will be celebrating their second birthday on Christmas day." An Eskimo woman made the parkas for the twins. The boys were given most of their winter gear by Eskimos and Indians whom Jim served as the twins were growing up.

Shortly after Jim bought his own plane, Millie took over the bookkeeping for their fledgling business. She shopped for their customers in the Alaska Bush. She bought mining machinery parts, food staples, clothes, and supplies women needed like material and thread. When Jim brought a piece of mining equipment in from a mine to be repaired, Millie took it to the machine shop and stood by waiting until it was fixed. She knew that every day a mine had to shut down, waiting for a part to be repaired, meant a loss of thousands of dollars.

Bush pilots cannot stay in business without someone to provide management and customer service. With Jim flying every daylight hour he could, Millie became his perfect partner on the ground.

Bundling the twins up in their mukluks and parkas, Millie drove to the bank to deposit the gold Jim flew in from the mines. When she took the twins into the bank and sat them on the floor with their backs against the counter, she left all the gold lying on the seat of her unlocked car.

It was safe to leave the gold in her car. In such a small town everyone knew all about everyone else—where they were and what they were doing. And there was no quick transportation out of town. Also, it was easy to tell from the color and texture of the gold which mine it came from. So it could be easily traced.

Jim brought the gold from the mines in leather bags called pokes. The pokes, each the size of a small drawstring purse, were so heavy Millie had to carry them into the bank one at a time. She laid a poke over her left arm with her right hand helping to support it. The bank gave her receipts for the gold she delivered and she sent the receipts back to the mines.

Millie also picked up and delivered freight and passengers to and from the airport. The twins rode with her until they were big enough to make pickups and deliveries themselves on their bicycles.

Millie made sacks for mail she collected from the Post Office and that Jim delivered to his customers. On the sacks she embroidered in red thread the names of villages and mining centers: Ophir, McGrath, Cripple Creek, Ruby, Arctic Circle Hot Springs, and others. She hung them in the hanger over the freight bins. As soon as they could read well enough, Warren and Jimmy sorted the mail and slipped it into the appropriate sacks.

At first all Jim had to house his plane was a nose hangar, a large canvas tarp that was big enough for a mechanic to work under. He and Millie made the hangar on their Singer sewing machine. All Bush pilots were good sewers and every one had a heavy-duty sewing machine. Planes by then were constructed of welded steel-tube and covered with fabric. Pilots and their helpers, like Jim and Millie, recovered damaged or worn-out wings by shaping the wing fabric and fastening it to the frame with a glue called "dope." Then they stitched it with long curved needles around the wing struts. And they made wing covers. Millie and Jim and their mechanic sat at a long folding table, stitching the tapes used to tie the covers on.

Getting a plane ready for the night in winter was a long cold job. First the oil had to be drained from the engine so it would not solidify. Then the wing covers had to be tied on to protect the wings from a frost covering, which would destroy the lift of the plane. To start up the plane, oil had to be put back in the engine and then warmed by a firepot under the canvas nose hangar.

The open flame firepots, used by all the pilots, were a great fire hazard. Once in Fort Yukon, Jim's plane caught fire and all the fabric burned off. From then on he used a small oil heater and put it in an oil drum under the nose hangar.

Before the end of his first year in business, Jim had his own real hangar, a building big enough for three planes. He added a plane a year and hired two pilots. Alaska was growing rapidly, and the prices for gold and furs were increasing steadily.

In the short arctic summer of constant daylight, pilots flew nearly twenty-four hours a day. They grabbed their food on the run and catnapped while mechanics gassed or repaired their engines and wives or partners took care of freight and passengers. Tremendous stamina was needed.

Flying was a daily gamble with the weather, and unpredictability reigned in every aspect of the business. Once when he was flying through a light snowstorm, Jim had to use one hand to help steady a passenger as she gave birth to a baby girl. Several other times babies were born in his plane as he was flying their mothers to hospitals in town.

When planes failed and pilots crashed, Jim joined the searches for them. After a week of looking for Frank Barr, who was lost in the Forty Mile mining area near the Canadian border, Jim found him on a mountaintop. Barr was hungry and exhausted but determined to return to repair his plane and fly again. Once an Alaska Bush pilot, always one.

World War II ended the pioneering era of Alaska aviation when the few Bush pilots flying in the Territory were household names and heroes to everyone. Their days of daring and glory, when aerial maps were unknown and sophisticated navigational equipment nonexistent, began in the mid-1920s and lasted less than twenty years.

In December, 1941, the Japanese bombed Pearl Harbor, Hawaii. Soon after, Japanese planes dropped bombs on Dutch Harbor in Alaska's Aleutian Islands. In the middle of the night Millie's sister called from an army base where she worked to tell her that boatloads of Japanese soldiers had landed on Attu Island at the tip of the Aleutians. Alaskans feared an invasion of the mainland. The Territory of Alaska was closer to Japan than to the United States.

In 1942 Japanese forces occupied Attu and Kiska islands. It was the first land invasion of the United States since the British burned Washington, D.C., in 1814. All that summer Millie kept an emergency pack with food, water, mosquito nets, and an axe ready in case Fairbanks was bombed or invaded. She sent the twins out to a farm in Washington State.

The Alaska Bush airlines were commandeered by the U.S. Army to fly military personnel and supplies to build huge airfields in Alaska. Jim still served his scattered customers, but by the end of 1942 most mines were shut down and the market for furs was gone. By 1943 the Japanese were driven from the Territory.

But the U.S. Army stayed on. The soldiers were strangers to the pioneers. The roadhouses that were near army bases were no longer family-style gathering places for miners, trappers, and traders, but instead rowdy partying centers jammed with "G.I.s." In 1945 Jim brought home from the roadhouse in Ruby a three-year-old girl whom he and Millie adopted and named Abigail. Her Athapaskan Indian mother had left with a soldier and her Irish miner father had died.

Immediately after the war, in 1946, Jim and several other small airline operators pooled their businesses to form Northern Consolidated Airlines, which later merged into the new Wien Alaska Airlines. Jim's commercial flying days were over but he was not grounded. He and Millie kept their private plane. It no longer reeked of the pungent odor of dried fish and raw furs and it was far safer and more comfortable. But flying wasn't as much fun with all the new equipment and rules and regulations, Jim said.

Alaskan aviation has grown greatly in scale since World War

II and Jim Dodson's pioneering flights into the Bush. Today Anchorage International Airport is one of the world's busiest, a hub of transpacific jet travel. But Bush Alaska, including the western half of the state which is larger than Texas and has no highways, is still served by small air-taxi companies. There are approximately two hundred for this area and they operate mostly small propeller planes, ranging from four-to-six-passenger Cessnas to nineteen-passenger Twin Otters. Service is by schedule or charter. Many offer "flightseeing" tours over mountains, glaciers, and bays.

Regular air service has bound Alaskans together and established the state's modern identity. The capital, Juneau, in southeastern Alaska, is far from the population centers of Anchorage and Fairbanks. No roads connect it with any other towns. Without air service, isolated Juneau could not continue to serve as the state's capital. In other far-removed corners of Alaska, air cargo and mail service bring everything from snowmobiles to frozen foods to the Bush villages.

In the twentieth century, air travel has become Alaska's vital bloodline. One out of every forty-two Alaskans is a pilot, eight times the national average. There is one plane for every fifty-eight state residents, which is fourteen times the national average. Flying in Alaska's extreme weather conditions can still be hazardous, but Jim Dodson's spirit lives on in the hardy Bush pilots who continue to connect the remote parts of Alaska, lifting passengers and cargo over the immensities of The Great Land.

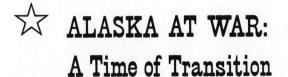

☆ ALASKA AT WAR:
A Time of Transition

World War II thrust Alaska on to the world stage and, in doing so, transformed the territory. As thousands of troops flooded in, construction boomed. The most important and lasting effect of the war was one of the greatest engineering accomplishments of the century. Alaska was finally connected by road through Canada to the rest of the country. Ironically, when the 1,400-mile Alaska Highway was completed, in record time, it was unnecessary for the war effort.

But at the beginning of the war, after the Japanese attacked Pearl Harbor in December, 1941, an invasion of Alaska seemed very possible. The territory was vulnerable: Its shipping lanes were open to enemy attack and it was inaccessible by land to the United States.

So President Franklin Roosevelt decided that, in order to safeguard military supply lines, a road to Alaska through Canada must be built as soon as possible. No resources were to be spared.

In March, 1942, the great struggle to blaze an inland pioneer road began. Seven U.S. regiments totaling over 10,000 men were positioned at points in the rugged, mountainous terrain of British Columbia and the Yukon Territory.

A few supply lines into this area already existed. Rail links ended at Dawson Creek and Whitehorse, the extremities of the route. Canadian airfields, built in 1941 for defense purposes, were to be linked by the road. But the army engineers faced a largely unexplored and unoccupied wilderness.

Road work on the "truck trail" was often an ordeal. Temperatures on the northernmost parts of the route in winter dropped as low as seventy degrees below zero, and the equipment did not work in the cold. Men died of exposure and in accidents. Work literally bogged down when the top ground layer was stripped off and the permafrost below thawed into a mire.

In the summer, mosquitoes and black flies were thick, and their bites caused bad swellings. The land that the troops pushed through was laced with rivers, swamps, streams, and lakes. One hundred and thirty-three bridges and 8,000 culverts were constructed for crossings.

At last on October 20, 1942, crews working south from Alaska and north from Whitehorse met at Beaver Creek, Yukon, just over the Alaskan border, to join the last sections of the road. It was cleared in the incredibly short time of eight and a half months.

The Alaska-Canada Military Highway, a grand name for the narrow dirt road, now stretched from Dawson Creek in the south 1,200 miles northwest through British Columbia and

Yukon Territory to the Alaskan border. From there it ran 200 miles farther on to Fairbanks.

But the road was rough and vulnerable to freezes and floodings. The work was far from over. Through 1943, the "Alcan" was upgraded and widened. Alaska was at last linked to the United States by a year-round passable route.

As the U.S. Army raced to open the overland connection to Alaska, the Japanese Army struck by sea. In June, 1942, hoping to divert American forces away from strategic Midway Island in the mid-Pacific, Japanese troops landed on Attu and Kiska.

Attu and Kiska are two desolate Northern Pacific islands at the end of the long Aleutian chain, about a thousand miles from the Alaskan mainland. Not since the War of 1812, when the British burned Washington, D.C., had a foreign country occupied American territory. But the Japanese held their Aleutian toehold for only fourteen months.

It was a three-sided war in the Aleutians—the Japanese and the Americans battled each other, and both fought the often brutal weather. Fierce storms, high seas, and raging winds, as well as the fog and cold, took their toll. The Americans continually bombed the occupied islands in an attempt to dislodge the invaders. Finally, in May, 1943, 11,000 American troops landed on Attu to launch a counterattack on Attu against the Japanese forces of 2,600.

For weeks the combat was fierce as the Japanese fell back across the rocky terrain. They fought almost to the last man. When cornered, hundreds committed suicide rather than surrender. In the end, only twenty-nine Japanese were captured. The Americans had lost 549 men recapturing Attu in some of the bloodiest fighting of the Pacific war. Two months later, the Japanese Navy escaped in foggy weather with the occupying forces from Kiska.

45 ★

Alaska's remote islands were liberated, and there was no more fighting on American soil. But after the great bloodshed of its recapture, Attu today remains one of America's bleakest and least-visited outposts. Unexploded Japanese shells still make parts of the island unsafe.

As the tide turned against the Japanese in the Pacific, Alaska became an important support base for the war in Europe. America's new Russian allies desperately needed fighter planes to help roll back Hitler's onslaught. The planes were flown up to Alaska from Montana via the Northwest Staging Route, which followed the Canadian airbases along the Alaska Highway to the terminus of Fairbanks.

In Fairbanks, Soviet pilots picked up the planes to fly across the Bering Sea to Siberia and on to the Russian front in Europe. The Russian troops stationed in Fairbanks took advantage of their American stay to shop for scarce consumer goods such as shoes, cosmetics, and clothes. Not until the Gorbachev era would there be such camaraderie again in Russian-American relations.

World War II spurred Alaska's economic development. The small town of Anchorage, strategically located on Cook Inlet along the Alaska Railroad, began its growth into Alaska's largest city. An important military presence was established throughout the state that continued into the ensuing Cold War.

The war also pushed the drive for Alaskan statehood. Alaska had fought victoriously with the Union against a common enemy and felt closer to the rest of the country as a result. In the second half of the twentieth century, Alaska would change from an economically dependent territory to an economically important part of the United States.

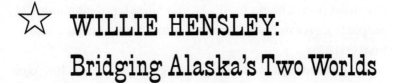

☆ WILLIE HENSLEY:
Bridging Alaska's Two Worlds

"I will say a little
about the way people lived long ago,
about the life I was there to see,
the life I was lucky just to catch
when I was a boy."

"The Way They Lived Long Ago"
Told by Tom Imgalrea

I n the time span of history, it was only yesterday that white people arrived in Alaska. Today there still are some Alaskan Natives who remember the first time they saw a white face. They can recall a pre-Western way of life when Alaskan Natives were totally self-sufficient, moving with the seasons across The Great Land, hunting and fishing for their food.

The ancestors of these Natives arrived in Alaska sometime between 35,000 to 14,000 years ago. They came from Siberia and may have crossed the Bering Sea by boat or, later, walked over the Bering land bridge. Experts are not sure how the very first explorers made their way from Siberia to Alaska.

We do know that from about 25,000 to 11,000 years ago— for roughly 14,000 years—the two continents of Asia and

North America were connected by a broad, dry plain that stretched from Siberia to Alaska. The first large migrations of people to arrive in North America came across this land bridge from Asia.

These crossings took place during the last great Ice Age. Then nearly all of Alaska's mountainous northern and southern regions were covered with glaciers. But the large, low central area of Alaska was dry land. The enormous amount of water frozen in the glacial ice had lowered the sea level, and the shallow floors of the Chukchi and Bering seas were exposed. These formed the Bering land bridge, which led from Siberia into the huge central basin of Alaska that was flanked with glaciers. The name given this whole plains area is Beringia.

In Beringia, the new people hunted the woolly mammoth and other fearsome beasts. The tundra was covered with grasses and herbs and teeming with animals: large-horned bison, antelopes, and giant ground sloths; yaks and musk-ox; lions and bears; camels and caribou. Then the glaciers began to melt, the seas rose again, and the land bridge of Beringia was covered with water.

Once more Siberia and Alaska were separated by the Chukchi and Bering seas. Most of the animals of Beringia disappeared, but bears, moose, caribou, Dall sheep, wolves, and wolverines survived. And the people who migrated to Alaska remained: the Eskimos, or Inuits as they called themselves; the Aleuts, a people similar to the Inuits, and Indians of the Athapaskan, Tlingit, and Haida tribes. All these tribes have legends telling the stories of their ancestors and the fabulous animals of long-ago Beringia.

There was ample space in this vast land for all of the Native inhabitants. It was not until thousands of years later, at the end of the nineteenth century, when the great gold rushes brought thousands of Westerners north, that the question of who owned the land rose. Prospectors and settlers staking their claims declared it was theirs. The Natives, whose ancestors had lived here from time immemorial, knew that by tradition and usage the land belonged to them.

But, since Alaska was so big and even with the prospectors and settlers there were still so few people in it, the land issue did not come to a head until after the territory became a state in 1959. Then ownership questions had to be settled so that it would be clear which lands belonged to the federal government, which to the state, and which to private individuals.

Very few Natives had much of an idea what statehood meant. Most were in villages living primarily off the land in their traditional manner, which in Alaska is called a subsistence way of life. The Natives were not involved in the political process that led to Alaska becoming a state.

When the state of Alaska began to make its land selections under the Statehood Act, a few young Natives who had received some Western education, realized the importance of some historical facts: The United States Congress had never formally denied the title of the Native people to the land of Alaska. The United States had waged no wars with Alaska Natives, as it had with Indians during the Westward Movement. There were no Alaskan land ownership treaties signed by both sides, as there were in the other states.

So, in the 1960s, Alaska Natives organized for the first time and put forward their formal claim to the land they lived on for thousands of years. The result was a compromise called the Alaska Native Claims Settlement Act, or ANCSA, passed by the U.S. Congress in 1971. It offered compensation for the loss of lands historically occupied by the Natives of Alaska.

Forty-four million acres were given to them by the federal government, which, when Alaska became a U.S. territory in 1867, assumed ownership of the entire area.

ANCSA also divided the 44 million acres among the tribal groups, which were then organized into thirteen regional Native corporations and more than two hundred Native village corporations. These corporations were established to develop the resources of the Native lands. The settlement also included $962.5 million paid to the Native corporations.

The "father" of this unprecedented settlement act is an Inuit named Willie Hensley. Willie is a young man of unusual talent and tenacity, and he is an optimist.

"There is some controversy about the equity of the settlement," Hensley says, "but in the context of history, if we had remained a territory, the federal government would continue to control us and we would have no power of our own. Now we are 70,000 Natives with some money and 44 million acres of land, about an eighth of Alaska.

"We are learning to understand how the system works so we can have a say in it. At the same time, we are trying to maintain our Native identity and our values. It would be a lot easier if we lived only in the context of our own people, but we don't. I grew up in a sod house and we used dogs for transportation. Now we're in the machine age. And we're still in cultural shock.

"But our heritage is rich," Willie says with a warm smile, "and we must not lose it. We know how to live off the land—to hunt, to fish—how to survive in the Arctic. We have our families, our traditions, our language, and our land, which are so much a part of our lives. At the same time, we have access to education and the Western political and economic world to do the other things we need to do. So we can have the best of both worlds."

As a Native leader of his people, Willie Hensley tries to reconcile these two worlds. Never before in the history of the United States has an indigenous people been able to negotiate such a large cash settlement and to keep vast lands on which to work out a merger of traditional and modern ways of life. Willie's own story is an amazing example of Native adaptability in these rapidly changing times.

Willie Hensley was born in Kotzebue, an Inupiat village north of the Arctic Circle on the windswept coast of the Bering Sea. The Inupiats are one of the Eskimo or Inuit tribes. They lived in tents in the summers and sod houses in the winters, moving with their dog teams, as the seasons changed, to the best places for hunting, trapping, and fishing.

His father died when Willie was too young to remember. Then, when he was three or four years old, his mother went to Nome and he was adopted into the large family of his uncle, Aqpayuk, known as John, and his aunt, Naungagaq, known as Priscilla. While Willie was still small, John died, leaving him fatherless once more. And, except for a brief visit when he was a teen-ager, Willie never saw his mother again.

His adopted mother, Priscilla Hensley, took the little dark-eyed boy everywhere with her. For endless hours he sat beside her, on a log on the beach, in tents or sod houses, as she visited with other village elders, talking and telling stories in Inupiat. Safe within Priscilla's circle of love, Willie listened and learned about the *Ilitqusiat*—the Inupiat Spirit.

"The *Ilitqusiat* is our tribal spirit," Willie explains. "It is a value system, a way of behaving that includes cooperation, sharing, humility, collective living, and respect for our elders. It is our culture and our way of life that is tied to the land.

"My adopted mother taught me to be obedient and helpful and to use my common sense," he says. But most important

51 ★

of all, Priscilla taught her nephew how to "just be." Willie Hensley has never had an identity problem. "Others might have problems about who they are," Willie declares, "but somehow my mother made it clear to me that I didn't have to go through that. I could just be myself—an Inupiat.

"My childhood was a traditional nomadic life—the kind of life all Inuits lived before the machine age. I still remember the first motor I ever saw. It was a five-horsepower outboard motor for a boat. I had never seen such power!"

Willie's life with Priscilla and her large family followed the rhythm of the seasons. In April he would hear the honking of wild geese and tilt his head back to see the sky filled with great flocks flying north in V formations, the heralds of winter's end. Soon the lagoons and delta grass of three great Arctic rivers that empty into Kotzebue Sound, the Noatak, Selawik, and Kobuk, would be filled with nesting birds: noisy gulls, cranes, eiders, clamorous old-squaws, hooting owls, sandpipers, snipe, golden eagles, and loons with their lonely cries.

By May and June, with the ice breaking up, the men launched their skin boats to hunt for beluga whales, walrus, and seals. Especially prized was the bearded seal, or *oogruk*. The women cut the skin away from the seal and the men used it to construct their skin boats: *umiaks*, or single-man kayaks. The seal's organs were dried and made into durable waterproof clothing, elegant carrying bags, and other useful items. The meat and blubber were eaten.

Summers the Inupiats lived on the beach. In this arctic region, the sun barely dipped below the edge of the Bering Sea before it was up again. With all this daylight, Willie hated to go to sleep. So much was going on—hunting, fishing, berrypicking. Elders from other villages would visit and swap stories. Willie washed and hung fish for drying or pickling, helped check the fishing net for holes, and filled his bucket with salmonberries.

By October, snow and ice were locking both the sound and the land in a deep freeze for the long winter. Willie and his family moved back from the beach, now whipped with arctic winds, to the delta land of the Noatak River. During the short winter day, they trapped muskrats and fished through holes in the ice. During the long winter nights, they were snug in their sod house dug into the earth near a stand of small, white birch trees.

One fall Willie got a terrible toothache. His family had already crossed the ten-mile inlet of water between Kotzebue and the mainland by boat and settled for the winter at Little Noatak. Now the ice had closed the water passage. But it was surface ice and not yet strong enough to hold a sled and the five dogs needed to pull it. In an agony of pain, Willie had to wait for the ice to harden so they could cross back to Kotzebue where there was a doctor.

Every day his older "brother," Aaron, tested the ice. Every day Willie's teeth hurt more. Finally, after several weeks, they ventured out onto the ice with Willie in the sled, silently crying from pain. Aaron walked ahead of the dogs, every few steps testing the ice with a pole, as they inched across the inlet to Kotzebue.

There was no dentist in the village, but the doctor looked in Willie's swollen mouth and decided to pull two teeth. Willie has never forgotten how much that hurt.

When he was twelve, Willie went with the men on his first beluga whale hunt. His job was to run the outboard motor as they chased the whale. When they were close enough, one man would first shoot the whale with a rifle and then the others would throw their harpoons attached to strong lines used to tie the whale fast to the boat.

"We waited on the shore, watching for the whales to go through the channel," Willie remembered. "You can see them spouting.

"All I was told was to steer the boat in the direction that the man with the gun would point it. When the whales came, we launched the boat and chased them. I tried to steer the way the hunter was pointing his rifle, but I was so excited I nearly drove the boat right up onto the back of the whale. It was about fifteen feet long. We got the whale and I didn't capsize the boat. But, was I excited!" Willie laughs at the memory.

Inuits have hunted whales in small skin boats for centuries. In the 1800s they began to see an occasional Western whaling vessel off the coast of Kotzebue bound for the Arctic Ocean. Then, in 1898, the gold rush to Nome that brought thousands of white gold seekers to the Bering Sea coast spilled over into the Kotzebue area.

During 1889 and 1899, about 800 miners from Nome moved north to the Kobuk River. The Inuits remember, through their stories, how they told the white men not to try to cross the river, but the miners did not listen. Many of them drowned, and others starved or died of the cold.

Kotzebue saw fewer white people than most coastal villages. The Quakers sent three missionaries at the turn of the century and when Willie was small, he worked for a Baptist minister, Dick Miller. Willie carried out Miller's slop buckets (there was no indoor plumbing). The preacher remembers that Willie worked hard all the time and always had money. Willie's relatives even borrowed from the boy.

Because Willie had lived so much out in the country, he was shy when he came to Kotzebue to go to school. He was a year late entering the first grade, but he quickly rose to the head of his class. Dick Miller noted Willie's intelligence and determination to succeed. Willie stayed at the head of his class through the eight grades taught at Kotzebue Day School.

At that time, if Native teen-agers wanted to go to high school, they had to leave their villages and go to a boarding school run by the U.S. Bureau of Indian Affairs. But Willie broke with that tradition, with the help of Dick Miller, and went to Harrison Chilhowee Academy, a Baptist boarding school in Tennessee. "I loved football," Willie remembers. "I was co-captain of the Harrison Chilhowee football team and played halfback for three years.

"I was barely fourteen when I left home. I was away four years and only came home once. But I didn't have any problems in Tennessee. I knew who I was." And he is quick to credit his mother, Priscilla, for his Inupiat spirit that sustained him in this strange white world. When Willie was not on the football field, he kept his head in his books, learning and waiting to see what life would hold for him.

During Willie's one visit home, Alaska was admitted to the Union. It was 1959 and he was sixteen years old. "I was in Fairbanks," Willie recalled. "There were big celebrations and I participated in all the festivities, but I didn't really understand what it meant. Nor did most Natives. Those outside the urban areas had very little idea what was happening. Promises had been made for protection of our land, so those Natives who were aware of it supported Statehood. But I was still a kid."

After graduating from boarding school, Willie attended the University of Alaska for two years. Then, "because at the time I didn't think much was happening in Alaska," he went back Outside to earn his Bachelor of Arts in political science at George Washington University in Washington, D.C. He studied Russian for two years and made a trip to Poland and Russia with the Experiment in International Living. By now he had grown into a slim, handsome, and athletic young man who seemed at ease in either a Western or Native world.

"But I couldn't identify with the Pilgrims, if you know what I mean," Willie says. "The focal point of my life has always been my region."

So Willie went home to explore again the rights of Alaska Natives to their land. When he was twenty-four, he wrote a paper titled, "What Rights to Land Have the Alaska Natives?" It was the first statement of the historical, legal, and moral arguments that led to the passage of ANCSA, the Alaska Native Claims Settlement Act.

"The state was interested because we had claims to the land that clouded titles for oil leases and for building a pipeline," Willie explained. "Without a resolution of the issue of land ownership in Alaska, the state could not proceed with any oil development."

With his nephew, Willie founded NANA, or Northwest Alaska Native Association. NANA is the regional corporation which administers the Northwest lands deeded under ANCSA to the Inuit shareholders. It is a multimillion-dollar organization, and Willie Hensley became its president. He also helped organize and became president of the United Bank of Alaska, the first Native-owned bank in the state, and Alaska United Drilling, a Native-controlled oil drilling company.

With dizzying rapidity, Willie Hensley moved from a subsistence way of life on the Bering Sea coast to that of a successful corporate businessman sitting at a large desk in his sleek, modern office in Anchorage, the largest city in Alaska.

His career has had a strong impact on the land he grew up in, and his sense of mission to protect Native rights has never slackened. Realizing that Natives need influence in the political arena to protect their interests, Willie helped found the

Alaska Federation of Natives. For several years he was chairman of the Democratic Party in Alaska, and he has served in both houses of the state legislature.

As president of the NANA corporation, Willie went to Russia to look at reindeer herds with the idea of introducing them into Alaska. Seeing the potential for Inuit employment for the next hundred years or more, he helped develop the Red Dog Mine on Inupiat land where there are the largest lead and zinc deposits in the world. When the Inuit Circumpolar Conference, an international organization of Eskimos, was formed, Willie was the delegate from Alaska. In 1980 the Rockefeller Foundation gave him an award for public service. It seemed as if Willie Hensley never slept.

Now, after all the frenetic years of shuttling between the Native and Western worlds, Willie Hensley is taking a break. He is still the president of NANA, but he is back home in Kotzebue to refresh his spirit.

"Business and politics are not an end," he states. "They are simply a means. For us, for Inupiats, the primary task is tribal renewal and survival." *Ilitqusiat*, the Inupiat Spirit, has been temporarily weakened, he thinks. And he is doing everything in his power to help find and restore it to his people.

To Willie's way of thinking, seeking the Western world's goals of economic success has led to the spiritual death of the Native peoples—a loss of their tribal spirit, their language and culture, and most important, Willie maintains, their self-respect. His people are plagued with alcoholism and drug abuse, dropouts, suicides, and crime.

"Family life is being blasted apart," Willie notes sadly. "Kids hardly know what is right or wrong. We're still in cultural shock from contact with the Western world. We don't know who we are.

"The land given us in the Alaska Native Claims Settlement

Act is our spiritual homeland," Willie says. "But it rests in a corporation—a soulless entity that is designed for commercial purposes. What each Native group must do is take responsibility to insure that its corporation reflects the language and traditions of the people who own it."

Once any Inuit could find his way across the shifting sea ice by reading the stars and noting the wind's angle. The color of the ice told him where it was soft; the sound of the surf and the cries of seabirds led him through darkness and fog. His senses were more reliable than sophisticated instruments which lose their accuracy the nearer they get to the magnetic North Pole.

Now many Inuits have lost their way. "People don't like to struggle for survival," Willie declares. "They would rather have oil heaters than chop wood. But we shouldn't forget how to be independent, how to hunt and fish and use our dog teams. There won't always be oil and money. Our resources are being used up fast.

"But I'm an optimist," he says with his engaging smile. "Subsistence living is a frame of mind, a way of being independent. I feel that we have developed a philosophy that can accommodate to almost anything and still permit us to maintain our identity. We still have our language, our traditions, our families, and our own space."

Now that Willie is back on the cold Arctic coast where he began his amazing journeys, he pours his formidable energies into the Inupiat Spirit Program he founded in 1981. He is visiting all the Inupiat villages in the Kotzebue region. "We are like one large, extended family," he says. "We must help each other." Willie encourages the children to maintain their Inupiat language, to listen to their elders, and to live by the values of *Ilitqusiat*. He wants them to know that one can be a doctor or lawyer and still be an Inupiat.

At night Willie meets with the village elders. Looking at their wise, worn faces, he must think of his mother, Priscilla, and how, as a boy, he sat close to her on a log listening to the tribal elders of her time.

How proud Priscilla would be to see how her shy little son has grown up, and to hear Willie Hensley, the ultimate survivor in Alaska's two worlds, saying urgently to anyone who will listen, "If our people are to survive, they must keep and foster the Inupiat Spirit. If we protect our spirit and protect our land, we will endure."

☆ MARTY KELSEY RUTHERFORD:
Pioneer Daughter

"This is the inner secret of our love for Alaska, that in her devious way, some time or other, she has been generous in giving us our chance to do a bigger or a better thing than we had done before, or guessed we could do."

Mary Lee Davis
We Are Alaskans

Valdez, Alaska, is a very small town with a very big spirit. It has seen hard times and been struck by two great disasters: the great earthquake of 1964 and, exactly twenty-five years later, the great oil spill of 1989. But the people of Valdez have always rallied and rebuilt. There is no place in Alaska that better epitomizes the pioneer spirit.

This remarkable little town is where Marty Kelsey Rutherford was born. She is the daughter and granddaughter of pioneers and she has lived through the hard times and the two great disasters.

"But I wouldn't live anywhere else than Alaska," Marty says with a cheerful grin. "My birth certificate reads 'Territory of Alaska.' And I was eight years old in 1959 when Alaska achieved statehood. So I grew up with the state. I've lived through a lot that has happened here and now I work for the state of Alaska. And that is very special to me."

Marty is a vivacious woman in her thirties, with big brown eyes and a winning smile. She holds an important position in the Alaska state government as Director of the Municipal and Regional Assistance Division. Appropriately, Marty's work supports small villages and local governments.

"We are the rural outreach division," Marty explains. "The real, true definition of Alaska is outside the boundaries of Anchorage, where half the population of the state is concentrated. The cultural life of Eskimo, Aleut, Indian, and native-born Alaskans is far, far away from Anchorage, which is just the service seat of the state. The true meaning and heart of Alaska is in the Bush.

"I really think of myself first as an Alaskan," she declares. "Then I think of myself secondly as an American. Everybody I know does. Life is different here. Alaska really is another country."

As a little girl, Marty went fishing and hunting with her father, John, in the Chugach Mountains. They caught grayling and trout, and shot ducks, geese, ptarmigan, and spruce hens. "We lived a great portion of the year on the game birds and moose Dad would shoot," she recalls. "I still like moose meat better than anything I can buy in a store."

In the late 1800s, when Marty's grandparents came to Alaska, Valdez was the principal port for the territory. It still is the farthest north ice-free port linked by road to the rest of Alaska. In Valdez's early days, steamships from Seattle were met by pack horses in summer and sleighs in winter. They carried freight and passengers over the Chugach Mountains on the Richardson Trail to Fairbanks and other mining towns in the interior.

In the 1920s and '30s, the Richardson Trail was widened

to a one-lane dirt track for cars and eventually trucks. All winter it was closed by snow, but the Richardson out of Valdez remained the major road in Alaska until World War II.

After the war, when the Alaska Railroad and the Alaska Highway became the principal routes for freight, Valdez declined economically. Many familes left, but Marty's stayed on.

"Our courthouse burned down in the early 1940s and the court was moved to Anchorage," she recalls. "Ships came in only about two or three times a week. We kids were told not to go down to the harbor, we might drown. So, of course, we went. We watched the truckers loading freight and explored around the dock and warehouses. Valdez was pretty quiet and there wasn't much to do.

"But I was fortunate to be raised in a family that was politically active, interested and concerned. There was always something going on at home when I was young. I remember many, many times when the state legislator from our district was pounding on the table along with my father and Bill Egan in our kitchen. Bill, who became the first governor of Alaska, was born and raised in Valdez. So was George Sullivan, who became the first mayor of the Municipality of Anchorage. Valdez is a pretty remarkable little town. We've always been politically attuned to what is going on in Alaska."

When Marty was young, the issue most hotly discussed around her family's kitchen table was whether or not Alaska should become the 49th state. "As a territory, we were basically without representation," she says. "I really didn't understand the pros and cons very well, but I learned that politics were important and affected our lives. And I was lucky enough to hear the issues discussed by adults who were knowledgeable. I'm sure that influenced me deeply.

"I can remember the day we celebrated becoming a state as clearly as can be. Alaska entered the Union January 3, 1959, but we waited until the snow was gone to celebrate. It was 1959 and a pretty day in July, which was special, because it rains so much in Valdez. There was a parade and lots of food and fireworks. I had new white pedal pushers and a little red purse for the celebration.

"Adults were in a great mood and not paying much attention to us kids. We could run around as we pleased. People were giving speeches in front of the little white telephone building on Main Street. It was a great day, a real celebration."

Five years later, on Good Friday, 1964, Alaska was hit by one of the strongest earthquakes ever recorded in North America. It registered 9.2 on the Richter scale. And it destroyed Valdez. Marty was almost thirteen years old.

Marty, her mother, father, grandmother, and grandfather had just sat down at their big kitchen table for a special dinner of fresh shrimp when they felt the first shudder. Dishes rattled and jumped on the table. Everyone looked startled.

John Kelsey, Marty's father, knew immediately that the tremor was an earthquake. Valdez was prone to earthquakes. Perched precariously on a mud and gravel delta, the tiny port town lay at the foot of a large glacier. The snow-covered Chugach Mountains, which rose straight over the deep green waters of Prince William Sound, surrounded the town.

Almost instantly another tremor shook them harder. "Don't worry," John said. "It will pass."

"But it didn't stop," Marty recalls. "The noise got louder. Thunderous. It roared inside my head. I was sure that the mountains were falling."

The tremors kept coming, faster and harder. The kitchen cabinet doors flew open. Tins of canned food hurtled across the kitchen and crashed onto the floor. A heavy steel coffeepot full of coffee shot up to the ceiling, bounced down on the stove and up again.

The Kelseys' big wood-panelled apartment was over the offices of the Valdez Dock Company. The whole building rested on pilings driven deep into the glacial mud. Now it shook violently.

John shouted, "Get into the doorjamb!" As the floor lurched violently, Marty's grandmother tried to catch the coffeepot and was thrown to the floor. Marty's mother, Jeanette, flung her arms around Marty, and her dad hugged them both tightly under the doorjamb. Marty held onto her mother as hard as she could.

The sound of water roaring in under the building grew louder and the wooden pilings screeched and groaned. The two-story building was only a block from the end of the dock and the waterfront. It tilted farther and farther over. Marty was sure they were going to crash into the roaring water.

The violent shaking of the earth came and went, came and went for a full five minutes. To Marty it seemed a lifetime of terror.

The huge earthquake was also devastating Alaska's largest city, Anchorage, miles away. It leveled coastal communities and washed away the entire village of thirty-two people at Chenega.

Finally it stopped. Fearfully, Marty let go of her mother. Her arms ached. John tried to open the back door, but it was jammed. The Valdez Dock building was leaning at an angle. It seemed forever before John was able to free the door so they could get outside.

Holding onto each other, the Kelseys stepped out into dark seawater swirling around their ankles and splashing up their legs. The sidewalk was broken in chunks. It had risen three to four feet higher than it had been before. John helped pull everyone up onto the sidewalk, then he looked toward the waterfront. "My God!" he cried. "The docks are gone!" They all stared in disbelief.

Only twenty minutes earlier John Kelsey had been on the loading dock saying good-bye to his old friend, the captain of the huge freighter, the S.S. *Chena*. They had just completed the paperwork for the *Chena*'s docking. John and his brother, like their father before them, owned the Valdez Dock Company.

Immediately John thought of all the other people who had been on the dock when he left: longshoremen, wives and children, families who had come to watch the *Chena* dock. He knew them all. They were friends. He had seen one of their closest family friends, the high school coach, and his two little boys standing on the dock watching the *Chena*. Where they had stood there now was nothing but roiling, angry water. The wreckage of the dock, the warehouses, pilings, and broken boats was tossing on the huge waves. The people were gone.

Incredibly, out in the bay, the steel-hulled *Chena* was still afloat. Three times it had been sucked to the bottom of the Sound and thrown back up by enormous waves with its crew still alive. Now smoke was coming from its stack and it seemed to be steaming through the cannery building that had been ripped from its pilings and was floating far out in the bay. One hundred feet above tidewater, trees lay on the ground, felled by the high sea waves that had destroyed the docks and buildings.

Already a huge fire was blazing at the fuel storage tanks by the waterfront. The Kelseys ran for their car. Fear of more tidal waves gripped their hearts. Marty fell up to her knees in a huge crack in the earth. John pulled her out. Jeanette took the wheel of the car. She gunned the engine and rammed it up over the broken pavement.

Everywhere, people were piling into cars and pickups to get out of town. The women drove and the men walked cautiously ahead through the water, feeling for cracks and holes in the earth and guiding the drivers. Jeanette strained to see over the squid stuck on the windshield wiper. As soon as Jeanette, Marty, and her grandparents were on their way, John ran back to the waterfront, joining others to fight the fire and organize some kind of damage control.

Jeanette drove on in low gear. Hitting the gas pedal to the floorboard, she slammed the car up over broken levels in the pavement and fissures in the earth. Two tense hours later, Jeanette, Marty, and her grandparents reached a hill four miles from town where other townspeople had gathered. It was dark. People went from car to car asking about family and friends who were missing. No one slept.

Twice that night people told Marty and her mother that John had died on the waterfront.

In the early morning, Jeanette and Marty drove on to a small cabin about ten miles from Valdez. Forty or fifty people were jammed into it. Marty went up to the attic, lay on a trunk and braced her feet against the pitch of the roof next to the stove-pipe. At seven o'clock that morning her father walked into the cabin.

"My childhood ended abruptly with the earthquake," Marty explains. "It was the same for all of my friends. We lost people we loved. Twenty-eight people died. Our whole environment changed. We knew nothing would ever be the same again."

Valdez had been battered by three tsunamis, or seismic waves, whose strength was felt as far away as Hawaii and the Gulf of Mexico. The town sunk ten feet and slid nearly thirty feet toward the water. The Kelseys' $7-million installation of docks and warehouses was totally destroyed. Their business was completely wiped out.

But John and Jeanette Kelsey were determined not to give up and leave town. The pioneer spirit in Valdez remained strong. Even though the town eventually had to abandon its old location, most people from Valdez returned to rebuild at a new, safer site a few miles farther west along the bay.

First they salvaged what they could. Main streets were underwater at high tide, and sewers and electricity lines were broken. Silt had dried like concrete on the linoleum floor of the Valdez Dock Company offices. Marty's father told her, "Your job is to clean the silt off the first floor."

"It took me all summer on my hands and knees, chiseling away, bit by bit, at that awful, smelly silt." Marty grimaced. "We stayed at Copper Center on the other side of the mountains, and drove into Valdez for three days every week. We ate at the Army relief kitchen. There were no other kids in town.

"But almost everybody finally came back. We were the first family to move to New Town, Valdez.

"My friends and I who lived through the earthquake still mourn for that 'Old Alaska' when life was simpler and slower and everyone knew everyone else. Of course, it had already begun to change, but the earthquake was a catalyst.

"Afterwards our parents were incredibly busy, rebuilding and trying to get back on their feet. They had no time for us the way they had before. We kids grew up very fast from that time on."

The relocation and rebuilding of Valdez was a remarkable example of community dedication and extremely hard work. The town was economically depressed and in debt, yet the frontier optimism Valdez was famous for prevailed. Everyone pitched in.

When the Magistrate for the Third Judicial District, whose office was in Valdez, became ill, Marty was appointed Acting Magistrate. She was eighteen when she was sworn in as a United States District Magistrate—"just because I was available and had the most education of anyone around at the time," she says with a smile. She and her friends were doing the work of adults.

Marty went Outside to college in Oregon, but couldn't wait to get back to Alaska. Fifteen of the total of twenty girls and boys in her graduating class from Valdez High School went Outside and later came back to Valdez like she did.

After a decade, the hard work and optimism of the people of Valdez were rewarded. The little town of 1,500 won out over the bigger ports of Anchorage and Seward to become the southern terminus of the Trans-Alaska Pipeline. The pipeline brings oil from the North Slope on the Arctic Ocean to an oil terminal across the inlet from Valdez on Prince William Sound.

John Kelsey was a leading figure in organizing the effort to win the pipeline terminus and persuade the oil companies to build in Valdez. "It took a lot of confidence and pride in the community to take on a $2-billion bond issue," he recalls. "But Alyeska (the consortium of oil companies) has allowed us a tax base and stable employment."

Marty went to work for a construction engineering firm at the Alyeska Pipeline Terminal. She began as a clerk-typist and became a job coordinator by the age of twenty-three, with a dozen employees under her.

"That job had been held by an engineer who trained me for two months before he went back Outside," Marty remembers. "If there was an engineering problem up in the tank farm, it was my responsibility to go up there to discover what it really was. Then I had to handle the coordination between the construction people, onsite engineers, and the management staff.

"If I had grown up in a suburb, I probably couldn't have handled it. But I grew up with all kinds of people and I learned a lot about construction from my dad. And I had already had jobs with lots of responsibility.

"Alaska is a land of great economic opportunity," Marty affirms. "There is a chance for young people to do a wider range of things at an earlier age than they can do in the lower 48. The competition is not so fierce because of the numbers, there are so few of us here. The population for the whole state is just about half a million. Yet we're beginning to offer a wider range of opportunities because Alaska has a little of everything in it."

Marty believes it is essential to encourage a diverse economy. Like many other Alaskans who are aware that oil reserves are finite and cannot be counted on for future prosperity, she favors small mining programs and fishing. But her biggest hope is for the growth of tourism.

"Tourism gives people the opportunity to look at what is undoubtedly one of the most glorious places on the face of the earth," Marty enthuses. "That is something we can use over and over again. If we are careful," she emphasizes, "we won't harm our land.

"Even though we have a large landmass, much of it is difficult to live on. Our tundra and our arctic areas are delicate. They cannot stand much population or they will start to deteriorate.

"But our population will never get too big. There are not many people who can stand the winters up here," Marty laughs. "When you go to Fairbanks and other areas you start getting the tougher life-style. Fairbanks has some extremely difficult winters. Valdez has high winds and tremendous snow load. The total snowfall for 1989 was 560.7 inches or nearly 47 feet, the highest in the state. Southeast Alaska has an amazing amount of rainfall. You go anywhere up north and you get incredibly difficult temperatures, and a tremendous amount of mosquitoes.

"And people in Alaska do not live nearly as comfortably as people in the lower 48 in terms of amenities. A millionaire in Alaska will live in a house that an upper-middle class person would turn his nose up at in the lower 48.

"But those of us who were born and raised in Alaska are used to a sort of rough-and-tumble countryside. We're accustomed to a frontier atmosphere that is not found in the lower 48. There is a freedom here to be just what you want to be, and there are no class barriers. When you get away from that freedom, you find yourself missing it very much," Marty states with conviction.

Even though she has lived through two major disasters, the earthquake of 1964 and the oil spill of 1989, Marty's love of Alaska remains unshakable. The earthquake ended her carefree childhood. The oil spill, she believes, made her more mature and sophisticated. Before the spill, she thought that any environmental problems arising from the development of Arctic oil fields could be taken care of. But, since that terrible night of March 24 when the supertanker *Exxon Valdez* hit Bligh Reef after leaving Valdez's harbor and leaked 11 million gallons of oil into the icy waters, Marty has realized that is not true. The oil is still not completely cleaned up. The damage to fish and wildlife is still unknown. And the lives of fishermen and small business people in little coastal communities like Valdez may be damaged beyond repair.

"Now I know how prodevelopment actions can really make

a difference in individual lives," Marty says. "And I'm more sympathetic to the environmental point of view.

"The oil spill was a hard lesson, but I would never think of leaving," she declares with the spirit of three generations of pioneers. "Alaska is very special. It's like no place else on earth. It's my home!"

THE VAN DE PUTTE FAMILY:
Fishing Alaskan Waters

"Unique among American fishermen, they [Alaskan fish-
ermen] see the present as a springboard rather than a
roadblock.

You who mourn the lost self-confidence and self-
sufficiency of the American frontier, look here."

William B. McCloskey, Jr.
*Highliners: A Documentary Novel
About the Fishermen of Alaska*

Faith Van De Putte began her life aboard boats when she
was five months old. She grew up buckled into an orange
life jacket. As she toddled about the boat's deck, grabbing
lifelines and crawling over hatches, Faith gnawed on the corners of her life jacket the way kids on shore might chew on
the ears of their teddy bears.

"When Faith was in kindergarten and first grade we were
based in Petersburg (in southeast Alaska), where there is lots
of snow," her mother, Renee, recalled. "Faith walked to school
by herself. She put on her life jacket, walked up the dock to
the harbor master's office, left her life jacket there, and walked
on to school. Coming back after school, she picked up her life
jacket, put it on, and came down the dock, back home to our
boat."

By the age of eleven, Faith had mastered the basics of navigation. That was her first year on the *McClure Bay*, her parent's eighty-foot fish tender. A fish tender is a boat that takes the catches from fishing boats at sea and delivers them either to a large processing ship or to a cannery on shore.

When Faith was little, the Van De Puttes fished off their sailboat in southeast Alaska. They caught salmon with hooked steel lines that they hand-cranked, sometimes pulling up four or five salmon on a line. Each fish weighed forty or more pounds, and it was hard work.

Fishing like this is called trolling. Usually it is done from a boat called a troller, which is fitted with hydraulic motors to turn the reels. But, when the Van De Puttes decided to sell their sailboat, instead of buying a troller, they found the tender, *McClure Bay*. They decided to move their base of operations west across the Gulf of Alaska and to try tending out of the port of Kodiak, one of the wealthiest in the country.

Faith's father, Gene, took his first run on the *McClure Bay* without Faith and Renee. He had a contract to service a fishing fleet in the waters of Bristol Bay, west of Kodiak Island, an area which the fishermen call "Out West." Bristol Bay is one of the richest fishing grounds in the world.

"Anything west of Kodiak is big business," Gene explains. "There's crab, shrimp, halibut, cod, pollock, and herring. I tended a herring fleet in Bristol Bay on the Bering Sea. But never again! It's wild out there!

"My crew and I delivered herring to a Korean processing ship right out in the ocean. There was no bay. The wind was terrible. It was about forty miles from catch to processing ship. You look on the horizon and all you see are ships. They all come into this area. It looks like the Normandy invasion in World War II. Otherwise there is nothing there. Just ocean."

The schools of herring start in San Francisco Bay and swim

north very rapidly. During the course of their northwest run, the herring are fished in Alaska around Sitka, off Chichagof Island, in southeast Alaska, then in Prince William Sound, and finally in Bristol Bay.

The herring are caught by seine boats, which use large nets, or seines, with sinkers on the bottom edge and floaters on the top. The seine hangs vertically in the water, and the fish are trapped when the ends of the seine are drawn together or pursed. Then the catch is delivered to a tender, like the *McClure Bay*, which delivers the herring to a processing ship moored in the fishing area or a cannery on the coast.

To make sure that the herring will not be fished to extinction, the Alaska Fish and Wildlife Commission regulates the time allowed for fishing in each area. Sometimes it can be a day, sometimes just a matter of hours.

"You never know what's going to happen," Gene sighs. "You hurry to get where you think the herring will be and then you wait and wait and wait for the signal—usually in terrible weather. It's just like those land-rush days when everyone lined up and the gun went off. Boats run into each other. It's just wilder than hell, kind of like a war. But there's big money in it. It's not uncommon for a seiner to make a half a million dollars in a couple of hours."

The weather was threatening when Gene steered the *McClure Bay* on his first trip down the coast of the Alaska Peninsula to the Aleutian Islands, which form a thin barrier between the Gulf of Alaska and the Bering Sea. Gene, and all the other boats around him in this annual fishing armada, had no choice but to sail through the dangerous False Pass in the Aleutian Islands to reach the Bering Sea and Bristol Bay.

"There is only twenty minutes to go with the tide through False Pass," Gene explains. "It's a complicated route and improperly marked. On the Bering Sea side you get a big surge.

Waves can be twenty feet high, and boats can hit ground at the bottom of the surge. You hold your breath going down. With the surge and poor visibility, all you know is what you read on your radar. Boats are lurched and turned around. Riggings are heavy with ice and you roll. It's a bad scene.

"Bristol Bay is big league. Hard core. Big money. You don't take your family out there."

So in June, after the herring run, Gene signed a tending contract with a large fish company whose fleet of boats fished for salmon in the quieter Shelikof Strait between Kodiak Island and the Alaska Peninsula. Faith and Renee flew up to Kodiak to join him. It was the first time Faith had been that far north or on a fish tending trip, and she was excited.

"We saw a lot of bears on shore that summer," she remembers. "The scenery, the mountains and all, was great. The wildflowers were beautiful and we were lucky that the weather was good.'"

That summer, the Van De Puttes honed their tending skills in the Shelikof Strait, but the pace was fierce. When they delivered the fish to Kodiak every four or five days, they hardly had time to run to the grocery store before they had to be back out to the fishing fleet.

Because of the hard conditions, there were not many families fishing out of Kodiak. "But we've always thought it is a neat thing to work together seasonally," Renee explained. "We can fish in Alaska in the summer and be wherever we want to be in the winter."

When the fishing season was over in the fall, the Van De Puttes sailed the *McClure Bay* south from Alaska to the San Juan Islands, which are just over the Canadian border in Washington State.

Here the Van De Puttes have their family roots. Gene's grandparents emigrated from the Oland Islands off Sweden around 1910 and settled on Lopez Island in the San Juans. They found the soil and weather similar to what they had known at home, and they farmed and fished as they had in the Oland Islands. Gene inherited their land, and Lopez Island has become his family's winter home. Many other boat owners who fish in Alaska moor off-season in Seattle, Bellingham, or other harbors on the West Coast.

"What we really needed first was a shop and a storage place to work on our boat," Gene said. So they anchored the *McClure Bay* in the bay at Lopez Island, walked up the shore to their property, and began to build first a shop and then a house. Faith rode the school bus in to the little town of Lopez to attend school.

Now seventeen, Faith is a pretty, tall, slender brunette who is thoroughly boat-wise. During the summers, the Van De Puttes return to the familiar waters of southeast Alaska in Lynn Canal. There, at the peak of the summer fishing season, Faith takes the wheel of the *McClure Bay* for watches as long as five to six hours straight (a normal watch is four hours). She reads the sophisticated loran navigational system, watches the two radars, and charts the course of the *McClure Bay*.

Lynn Canal is a deep fjord eighty miles long and six miles wide in the Alaskan panhandle. One of the highest coastal ranges in the world rises straight from its waters, and mountains more than a mile high edge the fjord.

Sudden gales of treacherous winds and driving rains can sweep down Lynn Canal, forcing fishing boats to shelter in safe harbors. Dense gray fogs often inch silently down from the mountaintops to the dark coastal waters, settling over the fjord like impenetrable eiderdowns. They make navigation nerve-wracking.

Faith, on watch, keeps her ears tuned to the VHF radio

where boats report trouble, ask for medical advice, and send messages. She listens for the weather reports and ship positions and is always alert for danger.

When the weather is clear and the air a deep blue, there is a scent of spruce and glaciers in the breeze. Snowcapped mountains and whitecapped waters sparkle in the sunlight. Then Faith is sure that there is no more beautiful spot in the whole wide world than Lynn Canal.

Nothing could be finer than those glorious sunny days when her father steers the *McClure Bay* out of the tiny cannery town of Pelican on Chichagof Island, through the tricky Iniam Pass, and then gives the wheel to Faith. He goes below to join her mother, who is catching up on her bookkeeping. The smell of their coffee wafts up from the cabin. Faith checks the instruments, turns the wheel, and heads for her favorite spot, Point Adolphus, where the whales hang out.

She watches and listens for boat traffic. Often there will be a large cruise ship coming toward her, bringing tourists from all over the world to see the glaciers in Glacier Bay. Faith calls on her radio, "Cruise ship coming up Point Adolphus, this is the *McClure Bay*." If there is no answer, she tries another radio frequency. A message comes from the ship: "Want to pass, port to port." Faith answers, "Roger. Port to port. *McClure Bay* clear." She signs off with her call sign, "WSD 2660."

Faith hopes the cruise ship does not disturb the whales and porpoises. "Definitely the best part about summer fishing is seeing wildlife," she enthuses.

Without warning, a forty-ton humpback whale will shoot out of the flat water with a thunderous roar, like that of a tremendous waterfall. A pair of killer whales, spuming torches of water from their blowholes, breach in graceful black arches. Flocks of white sea gulls follow the whales, skimming low over the water. The gulls are saltwater scavengers who cry raucously and snatch at the tiny herring surfaced by these deep-sea leviathans.

Schools of sleek porpoise dive down under the boat, then come up and sail over the water on the other side. Again and again they frolic from one side of the boat to the other in such joyous play that Faith laughs out loud.

"When porpoise play in front of the bow of the boat, they make a whoosh sound by blowing as they leap out of the water. The noise drives Pepper, our poodle, wild." Faith grins. "Pepper puts her nose through the hawsehole and barks madly at them.

"Then suddenly a bed of kelp around a point may start bobbing and swimming and you realize it's not only kelp but a bunch of sea otters as well. The otters hide among the long kelp streamers and their smooth little brown heads look just like the floating bulbs of kelp. The mothers float on their backs with their babies riding on their stomachs."

After the Van De Puttes have met the fishing boats, and all the fish that their tender can take has been loaded into the hold, Faith takes the first wheel watch. It is about a fifteen-hour run from the open water where the fishing fleet works, back to the port of Pelican to deliver the fish to the cannery. Gene goes below to sleep. The hired deckhand sleeps too. Renee finishes her paperwork. Faith is alone in the cabin in the dark of the night for the first six hours of the run.

For the past three days the *McClure Bay* has been taking on fish from a fleet of around twenty-five boats, each delivering to her once a day. Everyone has been working at top speed.

"I help tie up the fishing boats on the lee or protected side of the tender away from the wind," Faith explains. "Dad runs our two booms." Each boom has a halyard or line with a hook on the end, which is operated with hydraulic winches. The crews of the fishing boat unload their catch by hooking their brailer bags or plastic totes full of fish onto the tender's hook, one at a time. Then the bags are swung up to the *McClure Bay*.

Faith can take charge of this process: "If the waves get high or the wind changes and Dad has to bring the boat around into the waves, or if he has to go into the cabin to listen to or talk on the radio, I can run the booms."

Otherwise Faith is on deck, steadying the brailer bags or totes as they swing up from the fishing boats. It is a high-speed job. The Van De Puttes can off-load a salmon boat with 5,000 pounds of fish in twenty minutes. Gene reads the scale at the end of the halyard and calls out the weight of each fish bag or tote as he winches it up. Faith writes the weight down on her clipboard, then she trips the bag or tote to dump the fish into the hold of the tender.

"Renee is going as fast as her fingers can hit the adding machine, tallying up the amounts of the checks she has to write to pay the fishermen. We're dealing with different species of salmon that are being sold at different prices," Gene points out. "It's full speed. Then we pay them, cut the boat loose and they're off. And we bring in another boat to unload. Faith does the same jobs as the deckhand."

"Sometimes," Faith adds, "I have to help the other boats pitch salmon into their brailer bags or totes. Pitching is slimy, but I don't mind too much. It's my work."

On the *McClure Bay*, one of her jobs is scrubbing the fish slime out of the totes with a hose and scrub brush. She wears rubber boots and raingear. Once all the fish are loaded, she also hoses and scrubs the fish slime off the decks.

And it is Faith's responsibility to secure the deck. All the lines must be hung or coiled in the lazarette, a room in the aft of the boat under the deck that is used for storage. She brings the fenders aboard from the sides of the tender and puts them in the lazarette too. She ties down the totes, secures the hatch boards, and ties a tarp over the hatch in case of a storm.

Then Faith takes her watch and heads the *McClure Bay* for Pelican. As soon as they tie up at the cannery, Faith takes off the tarps and hatch boards and gets the deck ready for the cannery unloading. Then she jumps off the boat and heads uptown to do the laundry and see her friends.

The total high school enrollment in Pelican is only two kids, but in the summer there are about twenty other young people in town who work on boats, like Faith does, and she enjoys a break with them. They all go to Viv's Cafe or watch a video at someone's house or listen to rock music. Meanwhile the *McClure Bay* is being unloaded at the cannery and taking on ice for packing the fish on the next run out to the fishing fleet.

"Summers on Lynn Canal are great," Faith declares. "There are breaks between the salmon runs when we have beach parties with salmon and hot dogs. We go waterskiing and even swim, though the water is pretty cold. There's a place where a glacier comes almost down to the beach. And if we go walking in the woods, Dad carries a .44 magnum in case of bears."

For the Van De Puttes, family life is good on Lynn Canal. Their "neighbors" are other families who own and operate their own boats. The way of life they all have chosen involves hard work and high risk for the freedom they cherish.

The fishing life has allowed Faith to work at the full limit of her capacity from the time she was small. Now she has the self-confidence that is born of competence and experience. It is a true Alaskan pioneer heritage.

From the time she was eleven and began working on the *McClure Bay*, Faith has been earning wages. At first she made $10 a week. By the time she was fifteen, she had worked up to $25 a day. Now that she is more skilled and can work longer and harder, she gets $70 a day.

Since she started her earnings, Faith has bought all of her own clothes. Recently she bought a secondhand car, a 1983 Mustang, to drive around Lopez Island. With her savings, she plans to go to college and to travel. How long she will keep fishing, she doesn't know. But whatever new horizons are in her future, Faith Van De Putte will face them with vigor and optimism. She has already been to sea and stood her watches.

☆ SCOTT REYMILLER
& CAROL GELVIN-REYMILLER:
Life in the Bush

"Jan. 5, 1984   Came back from Birch Creek with dogs. Minus
56°. Snow machine wouldn't start. Long haul! Yeah for
doggies!"

from the Journal of
Scott Reymiller and Carol Gelvin-Reymiller

Carol Gelvin and Scott Reymiller met at Crazy Horse Camp on Alaska's North Slope oil fields at the edge of the Arctic Ocean. Here on the North Slope, in 1968 at Prudhoe Bay, the largest oil field in North America was discovered. Soon after, as in the days of the gold rushes, Alaska's economy boomed.

Large oil companies rushed to the North Slope for the new Alaskan bonanza in oil. Huge oil rigs were built. People poured into the state in answer to the demand for oil workers. High wages were paid to those who could stand the long hours in the isolation and harsh conditions on the shores of the Arctic Ocean.

Until oil was discovered, the North Slope had been the home only of Inupiat Eskimos. Few other people had braved the severe winds and bitter cold of the barren tundra bordering the icebound ocean. To attract workers, the oil companies built well-heated dormitories with recreation rooms. There were movies, and all the food one could eat was available around the clock—including fresh fruits, steaks, and ice cream in every flavor.

But the work was hard and the life was lonely. Most workers signed on for short stays of six to eight weeks at a time. Scott, a member of the International Laborers Union, laid pipe and assisted pipefitters and operators. Sometimes they worked in fierce arctic winds with the temperature at fifty degrees below zero and the wind-chill factor much lower.

Carol got her first job on the North Slope in the payroll offices at pump stations when she was twenty. "I didn't want to work in an office forever," she explained. "I had always drawn and painted, but it is hard to earn a living as an artist. So I thought it would be great to apprentice in the painters' union."

As a young woman, she might have had a problem obtaining a membership in the more competitive stateside unions. But in Alaska she quickly obtained an apprenticeship in Local #1555 of the International Brotherhood of Painter and Allied Trades.

Carol did industrial painting of metal: floors, pipes, structural steel. Wearing a charcoal-filter respirator to protect her from toxic fumes, she worked twelve-hour days. She sprayed valves and the insides of tanks to prevent rust (crude oil is very corrosive). For a woman as petite and pretty as Carol, working with an all-male crew could have been difficult. But she had the necessary stamina, plus an easy manner and ability to work with anyone.

"I really enjoyed it," she said with her gentle smile. "Ninety-nine percent of the guys in the trade were OK to me."

After the standard four-year apprenticeship, Carol became

a journeyman. She painted pipes and tanks at Arco's Seawater Treating Plant. Eventually she was made foreman of a crew of eight painters.

Carol was twenty-five and Scott was thirty when they met in 1981 after each of them had worked several seasons in the oil fields. They were married the same year at noon on the autumnal equinox, when the forces of the moon and the sun are equal. The dream they shared was to live in the Bush as self-sufficiently as possible and to be careful users of the arctic land they love.

After they were married, Carol and Scott continued to work several months of the year on the North Slope. Scott moved up the job ladder to welding and Carol to mural and sign painting. Sometimes they worked together and sometimes they lived apart in different camps.

"The reason we keep taking oil jobs is to earn enough money for all of our projects," Scott said as he swung his axe to split a log of wood outside of their cabin in Central. Central, where Carol and Scott now make their home, is in Bush Alaska. It is a village of about twenty people in the interior just south of the Arctic Circle. There is a store, a bar and a restaurant, a school, a community center and museum, and several old log cabins from the days of the gold rush in the Central area.

Carol and Scott's wood stack rises above his head and is as long as two cars. It is the only source of heat for their log cabin. They need to chop and split ten to twelve cords of wood to keep warm and to cook on their wood stove during the eight months of winter.

For an Alaskan like Carol, this seems a natural way to live. She was born in Fairbanks, but she grew up in Central. Carol had been Outside and to Europe and Africa. "But my travels have really been explorations," she says. "I've never doubted

Marty Kelsey at summer celebration of Alaska's statehood,
Valdez, 1959.

Marty Rutherford, summer 1977, end of the pipeline construction.

The *Valdez News* building, 1910–1915.

Robert Kelsey, Sr., on the Valdez dock, around 1940.

Arrival of the *Santa Ana* at Valdez, May, 1903.

Ptarmigan Roadhouse, Mile 31, Richardson Trail around 1900.

Marty Rutherford, summer 1989, fishing.

Faith on Lopez Island

The Van De Putte home on Lopez Island.

The *McClure Bay*

Faith celebrating her seventeenth birthday on the *McClure Bay*

The Van De Putte family

Carol with her team

Dogs sleeping in the snow

Carol and Scott

Front view shop/studio

that the North would call me back. I just consider myself *extremely* fortunate to live in Alaska."

Scott, who always wanted to go to Alaska, was born in Ohio. He is a quiet, thoughtful young man with a dark beard and hazel eyes. Inspired by Buckminster Fuller, "The Renaissance Man" who developed the geodesic dome and many other innovative artifacts and theories, Scott pursues a generalist's way of life. He tries to learn as much as he can about a lot of things so that he can be as independent as possible and take care of his own needs. When he went west to Oregon, he started and managed a health food cooperative. Then he worked on a tree reseeding project, learning timber and forestry skills.

"Scott is the most thoroughly conscientious woodsman I have ever met, and I'm picky!" Carol says with conviction.

Moving north to the Canadian woods, Scott learned basic survival skills. He lived in an extremely small and very light teepee.

When he reached Alaska, Scott began exploring the state by checking out the places he could drive to that were out of reach of the main roads. That meant driving down some narrow, disused dirt roads that had started out as trails.

Off one such road in the Wrangell Mountains, Scott discovered McCarthy, a nearly deserted copper mining town where about a dozen people lived. It was quiet, the trees were tall, the air was clear, and the scenery magnificent. Scott agreed to caretake a homestead there. He found he liked McCarthy a lot. It was the sort of place he was looking for, and during the winter of 1976 he built himself a log cabin there.

Scott planned to build a shop for his metalwork and wood carving in McCarthy. He was working as a laborer, but his mind was full of his own projects and he needed more time to realize them. The North Slope, with its high wages and short-term jobs, seemed like the answer. So Scott, like so many other young people from Alaska and the Outside in the 1970s and '80s, went as far north as he could go to work in the booming oil camps on the Arctic Ocean.

"But we don't think the simple pursuit of money brings much satisfaction," Carol says as she mixes a bucketful of dog food with cooked salmon for their six sled dogs. "It's *what* you do. We work toward increasing our skills and our knowledge. We're always curious and very consciously build our lives on learning new things."

Scott brought his axe to rest with a whack into the chopping block. "We really feel sorry for people who don't have curiosity or take pleasure in learning," he declares. "Alaska encourages diversity. Here work has a real purpose. You have to have lots of skills. The situations you find yourself in, in the Bush, call for constant adaptation."

Even with the demands of their do-it-yourself lives, these two young people manage to take courses in Fairbanks, 135 miles south of Central—Scott in mechanics and Carol in art. And like many other young people in Alaska, both Carol and Scott have earned their private airplane licenses. Recently Scott also qualified for his Airframe and Powerplant Mechanic's license.

Fortunately for Carol and Scott, they grew up in families who enjoyed working with their hands. Scott's grandfather had a plating shop and his father spent all of his spare time remodeling their house. Scott's favorite tool, when he was a boy, was a hammer. His father and grandfather taught him carpentry and shop skills.

Carol remembers following her father around their ten acres

near Central—"helping and getting in the way. I would blow away the sawdust when he was sawing," she laughed.

"Dad is the kind of person who can fix or build anything. Working with materials, now that is Dad all the way," Carol says fondly. "Mother can do just about anything, too. She is an excellent fisherwoman and hunter in her own right, and usually accompanied Dad. Her enthusiasm for the out-of-doors, the natural world, is really immense. I think she is responsible for what powers of observation I have, and her love of nature certainly rubbed off on me. My mother really is the most important role model in my life."

Carol's parents, the Gelvins, like most people who live in the Bush, do a variety of work, including mining and trapping. They live as independent of the cash economy as they can, hunting, fishing, raising vegetables, and doing whatever needs to be done themselves. Ed Gelvin can fix or fabricate any engine—tractor, car or airplane.

The Gelvins started out with a small cabin and a scattering of tumbledown cabins and sheds on their lot in Central. They enlarged their own cabin, repaired some of the others for storage, built an airstrip and added a large metal garage/shop/hangar for their caterpillar-tread tractors, tools, and airplane—the basic necessities of life in the Bush.

When Alaska became a state, land ownership and titles were established and land was not available for the taking as it had been in early pioneer days. So the Gelvins gave Carol and Scott an acre out of their lot with a cabin on it.

"The cabin was sinking into the ground," Carol recalls. "It had a sod roof. We numbered the logs, took the cabin apart and rebuilt it. We poured a concrete floor and got new windows and a roof."

They kept Scott's place in McCarthy, but spent most of their considerable energies adding on to the cabin in Central: a bedroom, a front porch, a back porch, and a woodshed linked to the covered front porch so they wouldn't have to go out in the snow to get wood. Then they began to make plans for a workshop for Scott and an art studio for Carol.

Carol keeps a journal with notes and sketches of what she observes in the Arctic. Then she refers to her journal when she does her drawings, paintings, and wall hangings made of fiber, beads, feathers, and other found objects. She uses pastels more than watercolors, she explains, "because pastels don't freeze and are good when you are out in the Bush staying in a grungy cabin." Carol has sold and shown her pastels and beaded fiber pieces in several exhibitions, including the All Alaska Juried Art Exhibit.

When they settled in Central, Carol and Scott were given a trapline by Carol's brother. Traplines were established through usage long ago and are handed down through families or friends. Now each line is registered with the Trappers Association. Every trapper has to buy a license, and the state regulates which animals can be trapped and how many, so that none will ever be in danger of extinction.

Trapping furbearing animals has always been an important aspect of subsistence living in Alaska, first for Natives and then for settlers in the Bush. It is regarded as part of the cycle of life in the North—an integral aspect of survival in the Bush.

Furs are warmer than most synthetic materials and shed snow better. Natives learned long ago that moisture from one's breath will not condense on a wolverine ruff around one's face in the severe cold. Today Natives, Bush dwellers, and dog mushers wear natural fur hats and mitts to keep their heads and hands from freezing.

Trapping was something Carol learned from her parents when she was a little girl. "My twin sister, Colleen, and I each had a little trapline," Carol remembers. "And each of us had a horse we ran our line with. Our horses would snort and paw the snow when a moose was in the area, so we knew when we had to get out of there fast." Like the pioneer children of the West, Carol and her sister went into the wilderness alone and, as she explains, "skinning furs was second nature to us."

"While skinning marten, I reflect on these animals," she once wrote in her journal. "How close they make me feel to this land around me."

In another entry she "reads" their bones: "These wolf ribs have many signs of his life—a slight lump in a rib—is it a healed wound of childhood? How did he get it? A kick from a caribou or perhaps a moose? Injured in a fall? I have a fascination for the animals. A reverence.

"Is it wrong," she wonders in her journal, "to kill these animals in order that our lives may go on? I don't think it is, so long as the proper respect for the 'soul' of the animal is there. Then what is proper respect?" she asks herself. "To me it is very visual. Display a small bit of the animal—a glimpse, an acknowledgment."

In her fiber pieces, Carol uses all parts of the animals: moose leather, caribou antlers, the tail of a willow grouse, marten bones. All of these materials were important in the lives of circumpolar peoples, the Inuits and Indians, she notes. "But since I am of 'Western' lineage, I try through my artwork to view the material in a way that really is a blending of the influences of my own upbringing: what I saw and what I had to start with."

Carol and Scott have two short traplines and a long one. One short line is a tight loop of about an eighteen-mile run and the other one is ten miles out and ten miles back. The long line is about thirty-five miles one way. "Then we double back," Scott explains. "On the long line we have a wall tent and a trapper's cabin to cache food and stay in. The first season we trapped just the two short lines with four dogs."

They use a sled and sled dogs to run their lines. Not long ago they bought a snow machine or snowmobile. They thought it might be easier and more efficient to operate when one of them is away from Central, perhaps working for a month or more on the North Slope, and the other must take care of the traps alone. But the snow machine doesn't always start in the cold weather. And if it breaks down out on the trail, there is no way to get home but to walk.

The dogs are Carol's special love. "At first we had twenty-two," she says with a warm glow in her eyes. "Then we cut back to twelve, then five or six. You start from a large number because you can't tell for sure, when they are puppies, which ones will be good sled dogs. But you have to hone down to five or six."

"Have to?" Scott quips. "With every new batch of pups Carol wants to keep them all. There are a lot of tears and trials before *she* hones down to six!"

Having a good lead dog is the key to having a good team. It sets the pace for the others. The dogs are controlled entirely by voice commands—no reins or leashes. An average sled dog is about sixty pounds of lean muscle, capable of pulling twice its weight. There is a brake on the sled that a driver can stand on to help slow the sled, particularly going downhill. But Carol, who is about 115 pounds, doesn't have much physical leverage against five or six enthusiastic sled dogs who might want to careen off the trail after a moose. She has to depend on her lead dog to keep them in control.

Picking that dog, who must be a leader and obedient, is an art. Then come long hours of training, establishing a rapport with the dogs, and teaching them to work together. This is

Carol's particular joy. She talks her dogs down the trail, encouraging, cajoling, commanding, always alert to their moods and wary of what might distract them.

Since they started trapping in 1981, Carol and Scott have kept a journal. They enter the temperatures, snowfall, their catches, and general observations. The journal is a valuable record. From it they can tell if the animal populations are staying stable or increasing or decreasing. The main animals they trap are marten, some fox and lynx, and occasional muskrat, mink, beaver, or wolverine. Carol's father taught her the painstaking art of sewing furs, and from the furs of muskrats, marten, and beavers, she sews hats and parkas of her own design.

Although winters are long and springs, summers, and falls are short, there are definite seasons in the Arctic. Even on the North Slope there is a summer season when the ice breaks for a few weeks so that ships can bring in supplies. Arctic seasonal changes are dramatic: from twenty-four hours of summer daylight to twenty-four hours of winter darkness; from eighty degrees above zero to eighty degrees below zero.

An appreciation of the cycles of life and a love of this land of extremes shine through Carol and Scott's journals. The following excerpts from their journals are samples of their observations. They illustrate the extreme variety of the seasons in the Arctic and the joy these young Alaskans experience living so close to nature in the Arctic. Entries by Carol are marked (C) and those by Scott (S).

FALL

October 1: Sunshine coming through—icicles on the eaves, frost falling off branches and the snow every-

where seems so bright in the eyes! Sun shines off
the snow and makes the underside of everything
glow. Anxious to get the dogsled out, but am afraid it
will rain again. (C)

October 20: Northern lights active. Twice tonight I
stepped outside to study the stars. I have taught myself the constellations. (C)

October 28: Saw a lone wolf while cutting wood. Had
seen his tracks the day before near the house. Very
little snow, so trails rough. Anxious to try out my lat-
est batch of pups. (C)

November 20: Warm, minus 10°. Took dogs and snow
machine up to Crazy [Mountains] cabin site. Spent
the night. Caught 2 marten above the site and 1 below. Northern lights. Beautiful view. (S)

November 21: Got up early. Had breakfast, then took
big runner sled up hill and beyond on ridges to right.
Hard going. Snowshoed ahead. Good on top where
windblown. (S)

W I N T E R

December 1: Scott is at Belenburg [their cabin on the
long trapline] for 4 days. It's minus 20° and the sky
is beautiful. High clouds tinged with pink and gold
and purplish gray. It's 11:00 A.M. and the sun is
low—hidden by the hills to the south. The hills are
dark blue-grays—the sun will roll along behind
them, setting the sky to glow, bouncing light off my
birch trees. Gold and pink birches. (C)

December 3: Early A.M. Still minus 30° [at Central].
The moon has circled overhead for hours like a big
shining eye watching this place. Moon shadows are
everywhere. (C)

December 8: The snows continue and the animal tracks
become faint, just shallow steps in the surface of the
snow. And I have this knowledge that all those living
things—flowers, berries, leaves and green grasses—

in seed form—are underneath the cold, white snow.
It's almost like a secret. I love that thought. (C)

December 10: Fur packaged up—29 [marten] in all.

December 17: Minus 15°. Went up the Crazy trail.
What a trail. Took 5 hours to beat over the trail.
Cleared some willows with the chopper knife. (C)

December 21: Minus 10°. Windy. Cut birch and stacked
in cabin [on trapline]. (S)

January 2: Warm. 10° above. A nearly full moon over
the Yukon Bluffs at 2:00 A.M. An incredibly beautiful
sky. Looked like a rain cloud of pinks blurred into a
sky of slate blue/gray.(C)

January 10: At 11:45 A.M. the sun shines in the far
window above my sewing machine and shines on the
wall where the wolverine hide hangs. By 12:00 noon
it has moved farther west and is almost obscured by
the hills. By 12:02 it is gone. (C)

January 15: Warmed up to minus 40° instead of minus
60°. Took all 5 dogs around Crazy loop. All traps are
A-OK—An 18½ lb. lynx in the same cubby [trap] as
caught 2 others. (S)

January 27: Minus 40°. Clear and bright with a wax-
ing moon. Shadows from the chimney smoke move
over the snow like ghosts! Moon shadows.

I go around constantly with at least 4 layers of
cloth wrapping my limbs—and not an insignificant
part being wool or fur. I justify eating more—have to
have those calories to burn for warmth! Other good
thing about severe cold: Wood splits easy. The scenery is some of the finest during cold snaps—crisp,
sparkling, still, and silent. (C)

January 31: 0°. Cloudy, slight breeze. Repaired snow
machine. Fixed cowling, muffler, motor mount.
Much better now. The sun is starting to make a difference during the day by about 10. Is light enough
to see by 8:00 A.M. Lots of snow. (S)

February 2: Minus 15. Clearing. Temp. dropping fast.

Checked B lines. Little sign except squirrel, rabbit
and moose. Saw ptarmigan. No marten. (S)

February 5: Staying several days at B cabin to do re-
pairs. Bears break in every summer. How to keep
them out? No way it seems. (C)

February 11: Minus 30°. Up Crazy [Mountains]. Got
my usual quota of 2 marten. Warm on top. Sky was
full of sun all day. Top of Crazys I lay on the hard
snowpack with my coat off, sunning myself, listening
to the little redpoles twittering below somewhere in
the spruce tops.

    Ptarmigan and grouse tracks are *really* numerous up
and down the trail. Also rabbit and moose. (C)

February 19: 0°. Seems like spring has sprung. Can smell
the snow warming. 30° above on top of Crazys. Hot!
One more trip out each trail. Then *Finisimo!* (C)

February 23: 5° above zero. Cloudy. Feels like spring.
Dark clouds look like rain. Got one last marten on
first set (trap). The wind did its spring houseclean-
ing. Dried mushrooms, leaves, branches and twigs,
whole trees lying on top of the drifted snows. Had to
saw several large trees out of the way. Set off [closed
down] all traps. (C)

February 25: Can smell the cottonwoods on the creek.
Set off Crazy line. Saw 2 sets of fresh marten tracks
at the top. One shat right in front of a pole set as if
to say good-bye and good riddance! (C)

February 27: END OF SEASON (S)

SPRING

(Carol's ideas for her artwork are all generated from
her surroundings. All spring and summer entries are
from her personal journal.)

March 10: Lovely spring day. Went for a jog with the
doggies—a fast ride. Stopped just short of crossing
the airstrip to the dog yard—heard an airplane. Sure
enough, Scott flew right over my head on takeoff.
Nice day for flying. Pups did great.

March 13: Snow is glazed by sunshine. Pussy willows are beginning and more birds are in evidence. In the 30s and 40s during the day, teens at night. Scott and I will fly to lakes to go ice fishing. Goody! Nice long blue-green skies last 'till almost 8:00 in the evening.

March 25: Got up early and went ptarmigan hunting with Scott and Mother. Snow buntings and chickadees are around. . . . *So much* daylight! This increase in sunlight never ceases to amaze me.

April 18: First rain. A welcome sound—barely audible on the metal roofing. Snow is disappearing fast.

It is 9:00 P.M. and the sun is still above the horizon—shining into our window looking west.

April 20: Snow is almost gone. Seems it might melt all night. It's midnight and I can still hear the dripping from icicles. Owls are active—smells are all pungent. Really spring. Snow is almost gluey, that sticky type just before slush. Warm enough to put the dogs' buckets out with water today. Won't freeze. Have seen a few ducks and the blackbirds came through.

SUMMER

May 11: Buds beginning to show green heads. Robins very active and vocal. Shoots of rhubarb showing. Got up to nearly 70° today.

May 16: Very cold and rainy. Sleeted today but leaves are unfolding and delphiniums and iris shoots starting up. Huge flock of Lapland longspurs were in the cottonwoods. They swooped over me low in a large mass and flew back to the trees. They sound like wind chimes rattling as they sit and chatter.

Thinking about Africa—being hot! How I would love to have a bright-colored bird!

May 26: Scott and I have our logs cut and peeled. Pad of gravel ready to pour concrete slab for the shop/studio. All this daylight! Can't waste a moment!

June 21: Solstice. Spent the night on Eagle Summit. Beautiful evening. Sketched and had a picnic. Saw an American golden plover. Interesting bird. Friendly and chatty.

Woke up this morning to *heat!* 80° in the shade. Summer is here. Everything blooming.

August 5: Skeeters [mosquitoes] have about disappeared and it's getting dark again at night.

August 19: Picked mushrooms again today. Lots of orange delicious and boletus. No shaggy manes as yet. A lovely time of year. The colors are almost too much to take in. The highbush cranberry leaves are turning red. Against the dark woods floor they glow with color. A few interspersed green leaves. Gray cottonwood tree trunks. It's spectacular.

September 13: A bright blue fall sky against the golden colors of autumn. The tall grasses are dry and fuzzed, fireweed stalks have gone to seed. I've often thought that birth begins in the fall with the falling of the seedpods. In death [of the parent plant] there is life.

At the far frontier of Alaska's wilderness, Carol and Scott are keeping alive the Alaskan pioneer dream of self-reliance and independence. They have learned to utilize modern technology while continuing to hone their handicraft and survival skills. Sensitive to how fragile and limited their beloved wilderness is, they treat it with respect and care.

Carol just completed her B.A. in anthropology, archaeology, and art. She is interested in the Beringian crossing of circumpolar peoples and is working at a "dig" of the Pleistocene period near Fairbanks. Scott is utilizing all of his skills of design, carpentry, forging, and engine building to do custom modifications of Bush planes for pilots with special needs, such as guides and the Fish and Wildlife Service.

They have saved enough money to buy an old Bellanca Citabria, a tandem two-seat aircraft that is not manufactured anymore. And they have finished building their shop and studio next to their cabin. They forego spending money on luxuries like indoor plumbing. Like many Bush Alaskans, they make do with an outhouse but own an airplane.

Now that the oil boom is over, it is uncertain whether or not there will be jobs available to Carol and Scott on the North Slope. But they have not lost the pioneering skills passed down to them from their parents. They know how to survive.

Comes winter, it is certain that Carol and Scott will be back on their arctic trails across Birch Creek and up the Crazy Mountains, setting their traps, cutting wood, ice fishing, and rejoicing in the exhilaration of running their dogs by moonlight.

"If I were an aboriginal person," Carol says. "I would worship the moon. It is such a calm and powerful light—that full round glow of northern light. It changes the long winter nights into a really beautiful world."

In the Alaskan Bush, the old pioneer dream has a new glow.

☆ ALASKA TODAY:
Oil and the Russians

On the clear, calm night of March 24, 1989, the supertanker *Exxon Valdez* ran aground on Bligh Reef off the southeast coast of Alaska. This set off the largest man-made environmental disaster in U.S. history. Eleven million gallons of oil spilled into the pure waters of Prince William Sound, and ended an era in Alaska.

For three days the oil rested close to the ship, then was scattered by a spring storm. Within two months it had spread 500 miles west across the Gulf of Alaska, broken up by currents and weather. A thousand miles of mainland and island beaches and coastline were fouled by slicks. Tens of thousands of birds and over a thousand otters died after being caught in the sticky waste. Some of Alaska's richest fishing grounds were closed because fish had become contaminated by the oil.

This environmental catastrophe was also a devastating blow to the credibility of the oil companies. They had assured the state of Alaska that they had comprehensive plans to handle a major oil spill. But when the accident came, the men and equipment were not ready. They could not contain the oil in the crucial first days of the spill, when it floated near the ship.

As the oil damage spread, Exxon came under enormous public pressure. It mounted a billion-dollar cleanup operation, sending thousands of workers to spray and skim the oil off the stained shorelines. Some workers even wiped oil off individual rocks by hand. But once the oil was dispersed, all of it could never be caught. Only 3 to 13 percent of the oil from the spill was eventually recovered in the massive effort.

Across the country, people were shocked by the accident, and many Alaskans felt betrayed. The effects of the *Exxon Valdez* oil on the ecology of Alaska's waters and coasts will be closely watched in the nineties. After the spill, oil development in the state will be managed differently.

For two decades, oil has been the most powerful economic force in Alaska, enriching the state and its citizens. In 1968, the largest oil field in North America was discovered near Prudhoe Bay on the North Slope. This led to a "black gold" rush to Alaska that was the biggest population influx since the turn of the century. This time the bidders for untold wealth, in the form of oil leases, were the multinational oil companies. The high wages they paid for drilling and construction workers led to a northern stampede of thousands of job seekers.

In the mid-seventies, Alaska saw another of the greatest construction projects of the century. Like the Alaska Highway in the early forties, the building of the trans-Alaska pipeline was a race against time. For three-and-a-half years it was delayed as its environmental consequences were fiercely argued in lawsuits by environmentalists and in congressional debates. Engineering safeguards to protect against structural accidents in the arctic landscape were designed.

Finally, legislative approval was given by the U.S. Congress, and signed into law by the president. The staggering expense of the project spurred it to be finished as soon as possible, so that the enormous profits from the oil sales could be realized.

The pipeline took three-and-a-half years to complete, at a cost of over $8 billion. The first North Slope oil was pumped down the pipeline on June 20, 1977, and taken out by tanker from the port of Valdez on August 1.

The 48-inch-diameter pipeline zigs and zags 800 miles south from Prudhoe Bay across the entire state. Over half of it is overground, and in some areas caribou can cross under it. The pipeline crosses the diverse Alaskan landscape of tundra, mountain ranges, forests and plains, ending at the Valdez storage and dock terminal. In the middle of the state it crosses the Yukon River over a bridge more than 2,000 feet long.

In 1989, the Alaska pipeline carried 2 million barrels of oil a day, contributing a quarter of the country's oil supply. At the end of the '80s, over 7 billion barrels of crude oil had been pumped through the pipeline.

Beginning in 1969, oil wealth swelled the state's budget through lease sales and production taxes. The state invested some of its billions of dollars in a Permanent Fund, a savings account for the time when the oil would run out. Since 1982, a portion of the earnings (not the principal) from the Fund has been divided each year among all the residents of the state.

The first dividend check to each individual Alaskan was for $1,000; the second largest, in 1990, was for nearly as much. Alaska has no state income tax; it is the only state that redistributes its wealth directly to its population.

Alaskans have generally supported development of the state's resources, and Alaskan oil brought fabulous riches. So the oil companies' claims that they could protect the environment in their operations were not examined too closely.

After the colossal failure in Prince William Sound, many Alaskans had second thoughts. Proposed oil drillings in the fishing harvest area of Bristol Bay and the caribou breeding ground of the Arctic National Wildlife Refuge were put on hold. The oil business would remain, of course, but it would not be as freewheeling again.

Alaskan history moves in large cycles, and one of the most exciting developments of the '80s was the return of the Russians to Alaska in the era of glasnost. The Russians left the territory to the Americans in 1867, of course, but they have never been far away.

During World War II, Alaska was a vital staging point for the wartime allies, Russia and the United States. But in 1948, with the onset of the Cold War, the Soviets stretched an "ice curtain" across the Bering Sea, where the continents almost touch. Eskimo families with relatives on the opposite coasts were forbidden to visit each other, as they had for centuries.

Forty years later, cracks began to develop in the ice. In July, 1987, a strong young athlete named Lynne Cox made history by becoming the first person to swim the icy waters of the two-and-a-half-mile strait between Alaska's Little Diomede Island and the Soviet Union's Big Diomede Island. (In the winter, one can walk across the strait on ice). The Russians gave the world-class swimmer last-minute permission to land on their beach, and welcomed her warmly on her arrival after crossing the international dateline. The following year, on his historic visit to Washington, D.C., Soviet President Gorbachev hailed Lynne Cox's swim as a symbol of the new links being forged between Russia and America.

Another big crack in the ice came in June, 1988, with a long-planned "Friendship Flight" from Nome to the Siberian coastal town of Provideniya. The 45-minute trip opened up the "back door" to Russia, which travelers formerly could reach only through the European side.

Upon landing in Provideniya, Alaskan officials were enthusiastically greeted by the Russians, and American Eskimos were reunited with Russian Eskimo kinfolk. One woman from Nome embraced a childhood friend she had not seen for sixty years. By 1989, Provideniya had become a jumping-off point for Russian travelers to Alaska, and by 1990 regular air service had been established between Nome and the Siberian port of Magadan.

The Russians were not slow to establish their own beachheads in Alaska, and soon they seemed to be all over the state. Hundreds of Russian and American fishing fleet sailors drank and partied together in Dutch Harbor in the Aleutian Islands. Alaskan and Russian scientists and doctors exchanged information on arctic human health research. Thousands of young Alaskans cheered a top Soviet rock group at a stadium concert in Anchorage.

In 1988, a Russian icebreaking ship helped in the massive rescue operations to free two trapped gray whales from the northern coastal ice near Barrow. Soviet Young Pioneers visited their Boy Scout counterparts in Nome.

Alaska is the part of the United States that the Russians know best, since it was once part of their own empire. Geographically, Alaska is much closer to the Soviet Union than it is to the rest of the United States. Alaska resembles the Russian frontier of Siberia in its climate, terrain, resources, and scarce population more than any of its sister states, and even shares a common Eskimo people with Siberia.

In a sense, Alaska is the Siberia of the United States. Alaska's hold on the Russian imagination was emphasized by a joke made by a Soviet official spokesman on a recent visit to the state. He declared that one cause of the Russian Revolution of 1917 was popular anger over the Czar's sale of Alaska in 1867!

The opening up of their formerly sealed-off neighbors sent Alaskan commercial delegations to explore Siberian markets and resources. Alaska's pivotal crossroads position on the Pacific Rim naturally led her to look west to the East.

Most of the state's annual billion-dollar exports of such resources as fish, timber, and oil now go to the booming economy of Japan. Korea is also an important trading partner. With the growth of the Pacific Rim production economies, Alaska's economic role in Asia will be strengthened in the coming decades.

At the end of the twentieth century, as at the beginning, Alaska is one of the last great wildernesses left on earth. But Alaska's boom-and-bust development in this century has brought the realization that even her enormous resources are finite and her environment is vulnerable.

Now the land is more closely watched and guarded by the state and the federal governments, as well as by the new Native corporations. Yet in the twenty-first century, Alaska will still attract those who wish to test their spirit with its vastness. This "great land" will remain America's permanent frontier.

☆ GLOSSARY

Alaska—Drawn from the Aleut word *Alyeska*, which means "The Great Land."

Bush—An area or village in the wilderness with no connecting roads. It can only be reached by plane, boat, snow machine, or sled.

Cheechako—A tenderfoot or newcomer to Alaska.

Lower 48—The rest of the continental United States.

Muskeg—Deep, swampy areas covering much of Alaska, where only moss, spruce, birch, and shrubs can grow.

Northern lights—Or aurora borealis, visible at night above the Arctic Circle in large shimmering arcs or sheets of various colors, such as green, red, blue, and purple. They are created when sunspot activity radiates charged electrons and protons which then collide with gas particles in the upper atmosphere of the earth.

No-see-ums—Very small gnats that swirl in swarms and bite creatures in the Bush.

Outside—Alaskan term for anywhere out of the state.

Parka—A pullover garment with a hood originally made of caribou or squirrel skin, or seal intestine, and worn by Eskimos.

Permafrost—Ground that remains frozen for two or more years. It underlines most of the region north of the Arctic Circle in Alaska. South of the Arctic Circle it occurs discontinuously, except in Alaska's southern coastal regions.

Sourdough—A yeasty dough mixture used by pioneers to make bread. Also a name for an old-time Alaskan.

Tundra—A flat treeless plain consisting of black mucky soil on top and a permanently frozen subsoil (permafrost) below. Moss, flowers, and lichen grow on the tundra.

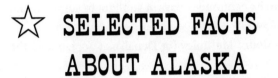 **SELECTED FACTS ABOUT ALASKA**

Size—Approximately 365 million acres, or 586,412 square miles, one-fifth the size of the rest of the United States. Only ½₀ of one percent of Alaska's land is settled.

Population—With 550,000 people, Alaska is the second smallest state after Wyoming. There is over a square mile of land per every resident of Alaska.

Natives—Approximately 34,000 Eskimos, 22,000 Indians, and 8,000 Aleuts make up 13 percent of Alaska's population.

Borders—The Alaskan/Canadian border is 1,538 miles long.
Alaska's 6,640-mile-long coastline faces the North Pacific Ocean, the Bering Sea, the Chukchi Sea, and the Arctic Ocean.

Climate records—Hottest: 100° F, Fort Yukon, June 27, 1915
Coldest: −80° F, Prospect Creek Camp, January 23, 1971

Longest days and nights—In Barrow, the state's northernmost community, there are 84 continuous days of sunlight in summer, and 67 days without sun in winter.

Tallest mountain—Mount McKinley (or Denali), at 20,320 feet, the tallest in North America.

Longest river—The Yukon River, with 1,400 miles in Alaska, 475 miles in Canada, is the fifth longest river system in North America.

Lakes—Alaska has over 3 million, mostly small, lakes. The largest, Lake Iliamna, covers 1,150 square miles.

Glaciers—Formed in areas where more snow falls than melts, glaciers cover approximately 30,000 square miles, or 3 percent of Alaska.

Earthquakes—On March 27, 1964, the strongest earthquake ever recorded in North America (9.2 on the Richter Scale), centered in northern Prince William Sound, spread shock waves extending 700 miles and killed 131 persons.

☆ SELECTED BIBLIOGRAPHY

The Alaska Almanac: Facts About Alaska. 1990 Edition. Anchorage: Alaska Northwest Publishing Company.

McCloskey, William. *Highliners: A Documentary Novel About the Fishermen of Alaska.* New York: McGraw-Hill Book Company, 1979.

Murie, Margaret. *Two in the Far North.* Anchorage: Alaska Northwest Publishing Company, 1988.

Paulsen, Gary. *Dogsong.* New York: Puffin Books, 1985.

Potter, Jean. *The Flying North.* Sausalito, California: Comstock Editions, Inc., 1986.

Shields, Mary. *Sled Dog Trails.* Anchorage: Alaska Northwest Publishing Company, 1984.

Specht, Robert. *Tisha: The Story of a Young Teacher in the Alaska Wilderness.* New York: Bantam Books, 1978.

Wilder, Edna. *Once Upon an Eskimo Time.* Edmonds, Washington: Alaska Northwest Publishing Company, 1987.

 **INDEX**